Son
of the mob

Hollywood Hustle

**GORDON
KORMAN**

HYPERION PAPERBACKS NEW YORK

SOUTH BURLINGTON COMM. LIBRARY
540 Dorset Street
South Burlington, VT 05403

In memory of Marilyn E. Marlow

I miss you

If you purchased this book without a cover, you should be aware that this book is
stolen property. It was reported as "unsold and destroyed" to the publisher, and neither
the author nor the publisher has received any payment for this "stripped" book.

Text © 2004 by Gordon Korman
All rights reserved. No part of this book may be reproduced or transmitted in any
form or by any means, electronic or mechanical, including photocopying, recording, or
by any information storage and retrieval system, without written permission from the
publisher. For information address Hyperion Books for Children, 114 Fifth Avenue,
New York, New York 10011-5690.

First Hyperion Paperbacks edition, 2006

1 3 5 7 9 10 8 6 4 2

Printed in the United States of America

Library of Congress Cataloging-in-Publication Data on file.
ISBN 0-7868-0919-1 (pbk.)

Visit www.hyperionteens.com

CHAPTER ONE

AERIAL SHOT—THE OPEN ROAD—DAY

An old Mazda Protegé tools along the cable
of highway into the brilliant sunrise.
With the rapid-fire blur of broken lines
on the asphalt, the weight of New York--
childhood, family, smog--recedes into
history. Every fiber of this scene, every
pixel, screams, "Freedom!"

INT. THE PROTEGÉ

VINCE LUCA at the wheel, girlfriend KENDRA
BIGHTLY, shotgun, and best friend ALEX
TARKANIAN in back. A handful of time zones
beyond the car's front bumper, new lives
as college freshmen await these three
young people.

Suddenly, a massive eighteen-wheeler zooms up from behind them. The diminutive rust bucket becomes an airborne tumbleweed in the slipstream. Bouncing along the pavement, the car falls apart like the motorized roller skate it was always meant to be, leaving our heroes to walk to college. . . .

"It doesn't say that!" I explode, clenching the wheel.

From the depth of my screenplay pages, Alex grins at me via the rearview mirror. "I'm just adding a little spice. 'New lives await these three young people?' Jeez, Vince, when were you reborn as a dork?"

"It's part of being a film student," I explain. "I have to get into the habit of seeing everything as a movie scene."

"The sun rises in the east," Kendra points out.

"Huh?"

"We're driving west. We can't be heading into the sunrise."

Not much gets past Kendra. She has a fact-checker's heart and a photographic memory. This sometimes makes it interesting being her boyfriend—especially for a guy with a pedigree like mine.

"Well, I'm just getting started," I concede. "I'm not exactly Scorsese yet."

"Bad example," Alex admonishes. "Isn't *Goodfellas* exactly what you're going to California to get away from?"

Leave it to Alex to hit the nail right on the head: my father's business, Brothers Vending Machines, Inc. Vending machines have precious little to do with it.

Penny's Motel in Vandalia, Illinois, is our first stop, fifteen mind-numbing hours from our homes on the south shore of Long Island.

"Remember, no funny business," Alex warns as we toss our bags on the two double beds. "We're here to get some sleep, not for you guys to do what comes naturally."

Alex has not shut up about this since the George Washington Bridge. My friend is basically a six-foot-tall hormone.

"You've got nothing to worry about," I assure him with a yawn. "The second my head hits that pillow, I'm going to be dead to the world."

Kendra goes to take a shower.

Alex watches the bathroom door close behind her, waits for the noise of the water. "Ah, Vince. Starting college with a steady girlfriend. Not smart."

"What are you talking about?" I say irritably. "You'd sell your own mother for a date."

"Yeah—in high school. College is where the playing field levels out. *They* start to want *us* as much as *we* want *them*. It's like peddling Sterno in Alaska. You can't miss—unless you're dumb enough to be unavailable."

"Just don't freak out if sales are a little sluggish at first," I advise him.

"Are you kidding?" he crows. "I'm going to be in Las Vegas! The whole city is built on money and sex. Frankie promised to show me the ropes."

"I didn't know you had a friend in Vegas."

"He's not really *my* friend. I got his number from your brother." He pulls a mummified cocktail napkin from the pocket of his jeans and painstakingly unfolds it. "Frankie Toronto. Maybe he's in the casino business."

"Are you crazy? You *never* get hooked up with somebody who knows my family. And that goes double if he has the same last name as a city!"

"Tommy begged me to look him up," he argues. "Frankie's one of his best friends."

"What were his exact words?" I demand. "Did he call the guy 'a friend of *mine*' or 'a friend of *ours*'?"

Alex shrugs. "What difference does it make?"

"Oh, not much," I say sarcastically. "*A friend of mine* means 'a friend of mine.' *A friend of ours* means a made guy who kills people."

"It's not like that," he insists. "Your brother knows I'm a citizen."

"Civilian," I correct.

"He knows I'm a regular person. He wouldn't hook me up with anybody dangerous."

"Trust me on this, Alex. I grew up with these wiseguys. I can spot the Mob a mile away. It's like a sixth sense."

I flip the clasps on my bag and throw the lid open.

And slam it back down again.

This isn't my suitcase! I mean, the suitcase is mine, but the stuff inside isn't! This is full of—

I peek again, hoping against hope to see my mother's neat packing job, an engineering feat that borders on the Cartesian. The perfectly folded clothes, the shoes stuffed with tissue paper, the toiletries filling empty spaces with geometric precision . . .

Uh-uh.

My luggage is filled with hundred-dollar bills, thousands of them, bundled in rubber bands.

And the amazing part? I know instantly where all this money comes from.

Loansharking, gambling, extortion, racketeering, and worse. Who knows? Some of it might even have come from vending machines. But I guarantee this: not one cent of it is legal.

More specifically, it comes from dear old Dad. Anthony Luca, businessman, father, Mob boss.

But what is it doing in my suitcase?

Obviously, this has to be some kind of mistaken identity. Two bags, one for college, one for my father. I have a giddy vision of Dad cracking my suitcase to find sweat socks instead of a zillion dollars. Or worse—what if that money was meant for someone else? A rival boss, who flies off the handle at this insult. Honor and respect are very big in that world. He could be sending an army of goons over to my house right now.

I've got to talk to Dad!

Alex is looking at me quizzically. "What's wrong?"

"Nothing. I—I'm going to take a walk."

"Why don't you just say it? You want me to get lost so you and Kendra can be alone for a while."

"That's not it—"

"Well, I won't do it," he goes on. "I'm paying for a third of this hotel room. It's all of ours, not your private little love nest. And don't think you can wait till the middle of the night, either. I'm a very light sleeper—"

"Alex—" I open the suitcase for him.

He goggles. "Jeez, Vince. I know L.A. is expensive, but how much money do you need?"

"It's Mob money!" I rasp. "I must have taken the wrong suitcase!"

Alex whistles. "How much do you think there is?"

We do a little wiseguy accounting. Hundred-dollar bills, four packets across by seven deep, stacked at least a dozen high. Three million. Maybe four.

I point to the bathroom door. "Not a word to Kendra, you hear me? For all we know, her old man's looking for this money."

That's the big kicker about Kendra: her dad is an FBI agent. Not just any FBI agent, but Agent Bite-Me, head of the Luca investigation. Of all the girls in the tristate area, I had to fall for the daughter of the guy whose job it is to send my father to prison.

Outside, I pace the parking lot, dialing my cell phone. As it rings, I'm racking my brain for the right words to describe this situation: *Hey, Dad, thanks for the little surprise in my suitcase*, or *I*

*might have some odds and ends that belong to
you.* The vending machine business is full of sur-
prises and odds and ends. Why can't I speak in
plain English? Because the phones in our house
are always bugged.

"Mom—hi. Is Dad around?"

"Vincent! Are you hurt?"

"Of course not. I just need to talk to—"

She cuts me off. "There's a twenty-car pileup
outside Knoxville. Dozens of fatalities. It's all over
CNN."

How's that for ironic? Dad spends his days
rubbing elbows with hired killers and the scum of
the earth. He's married to the undisputed world
champion of worrying, who wastes her anxiety on
imaginary tragedies.

"That's in Tennessee, Mom. I'm in Illinois. A
thousand miles away."

"Thank God!" In her eyes, that's a near miss.
"Is Alex okay? And how about that girl of yours?"

Mom has never once called Kendra by her
name. Which is still nicer than what Dad and
Tommy call her.

"They're fine. Just put Dad on, okay?"

"Your father's not here. He and your brother
are at a meeting."

It's almost midnight on the East Coast. Only

the vending machine business operates on these hours. "Just have them call me on my cell. Anytime—day or night."

"Vincent!" She's horrified. "There *is* something wrong!"

"*Anytime*—promise, Mom!"

I "sleep" with one hand clutching the suitcase. My cell phone never rings.

"You look awful," Alex tells me as we're loading the Mazda the next morning. His eyes narrow. "You and Kendra were up all night getting it on."

I whack him on the side of the head with three million dollars, maybe four.

At last we're ready to roll. Kendra gets in beside me and frowns. "Aren't those the same clothes you wore yesterday?"

If Agent Bite-Me had his daughter's eye for detail, Dad would have to be a whole lot more careful.

"Fifteen hours in the car, and you don't even change?"

"He didn't even shower," Alex puts in helpfully.

She calls me Stinky for the next nine hours.

TRACKING SHOT—INTERSTATE 45—DAY

A hulking SUV pulls even with the Mazda on the highway.

CLOSE-UP—THE WINDOW

The mirrored glass retreats into the door
panel to reveal . . .

The barrel of a Glock 9 machine pistol!

A hail of bullets perforates the
Protegé's rusty exterior, forcing the car
into the ditch.

Heavily armed GANGSTERS pour out of the
SUV. A burst of gunfire opens the trunk
lock, and the attackers abscond with
three million dollars, maybe four. . . .

When you spend the entire summer training
yourself to think in script form, your imagination
tends to get the better of you.

My cell doesn't ring until I'm in the bathroom
of the truck stop outside Columbia, Missouri.

"Dad?"

It's my brother. "Hey, Vince, how's it going?
You should've invested in luggage wheels. Heavy
bag, huh?"

"Don't joke about that, Tommy. I almost had a
heart attack, and I'll bet Dad did too."

"Are you kidding? You guys are right on
schedule. Now, here's my number. . . ."

"No!" I shout, but he's already rattling off the ten digits of the pay phone he's calling from. I have to find one out here and get back to him. Standard Mob procedure—the FBI can't tap public phones.

I have to buy six packs of gum before I've got enough coins. Next time you think small-town folks are friendly, try asking for change at a truck stop.

"Tommy's Mortuary."

"It's going to be," I growl. "Dad'll kill you if he finds out you've got me mixed up in this."

He sounds hurt. "The kind of money he's paying for that fancy college, you should be thrilled to help him out. Now listen: Uncle Bignose is already on a plane. He lands at the Kansas City airport at two-forty. Gate B seventy-seven."

"And he's got my clothes?" I ask.

"They're going by UPS. Listen—airport security won't let you in unless you're a passenger, so there's a ticket in your name at the Continental desk—"

"I can't get on a plane!" I explode. "I've got to drop Alex in Vegas and then drive with Kendra to L.A.!"

"The ticket's just to get you to the gate. Then you cash it in and keep the money. Buy yourself some new clothes."

"What for?" I ask. "You said my stuff's on the way."

"The FBI's got kind of a thing for that suit-case," he admits. "For some reason, they think it's full of juice. Flippin' feds."

It all comes together in my head with a jarring crunch. This was no case of switched luggage! The heat was on this money, and my Mazda was the only safe way to get it out of town.

"You used me," I accuse him.

He's offended. "What are you ragging on me for? Talk to your girlfriend. It's her old man who's sniffing through your underwear. Listen, Vince—gotta go. Have fun in college. Learn something."

He hangs up before I can unload on him. But it occurs to me that Tommy's probably just the messenger. Dad would never put his hotheaded older son in charge of this much cash. And anyway, the plan is too clever for my brother. To sneak the money past the FBI in the very same car as Agent Bite-Me's daughter—that's the kind of audacity that's made Anthony Luca the vending machine king of New York.

So much for his promise to keep my life totally separate from the business.

The irony is that no one could be more pumped than Dad about my going away to school. A taci-turn man in a world dominated by bigmouths, these days he can hardly shut up about "the first Luca to go to university."

"What was that all about?" Kendra asks back at the car.

I take a deep breath. "We have to stop in a couple of hours and meet somebody. It shouldn't take long."

"Meet somebody?" Her brow furrows. "We're hundreds of miles from anybody we know."

"I have something, and it's not mine," I explain, painfully aware of how much I sound like a scene out of *The Sopranos*, "so a guy is coming to get it."

But you can't blow something like this past Kendra. She has inherited FBI-agent DNA. What something? How did I get it? Why can't I just ship it back?

Finally, I say it outright. "I can't tell you."

She sulks all the way to Kansas City.

I have to drive like a maniac to get to the airport in time. As it is, we pull up just five minutes before Uncle Bignose's flight.

I hit the sidewalk running. "Don't park!" I toss over my shoulder. "I'll be right back!"

The ticket's waiting for me at the Continental counter, but when I sprint for the security checkpoint, Uncle Bignose's plane is already on the ground.

Wouldn't you know it? My belt buckle sets off the metal detector, and the agent pulls me aside.

"I'll just need you to open your bag, sir."

Not good. I am about to be caught with money that's wanted by the FBI. The spoils of God-only-knows what crime.

"I—I—"

That's when I see Uncle Bignose. He's not a svelte man, but he's pounding toward us at incredible speed, propelled by the magical attraction that can only exist between a wiseguy and a suitcase full of cash.

His collision with the luggage-check table knocks down three agents, mine included. A flailing arm snags the bag, and he bolts for the exit.

The total chaos that follows might be explained by the fact that airport security is designed to keep intruders *out*, not in. Suddenly, uniformed people are in motion, a mad scramble after Uncle Bignose's fleeing bulk. There's a lot of yelling too, but I can't decipher much of it because of the siren that's going off.

Trying to look just as bewildered as everybody else, I join the stampede. An announcement is blasting over the PA system. I think they're evacuating the building.

There's no sign of Uncle Bignose, but I do run

into Kendra and Alex. They both seem stunned, and Kendra is crying.

"It's okay! Some guy busted through security."

She's close to hysterical. "He pulled me out of the car! By the *hair*!"

"Who did?"

"The *guy*!" Alex is shaken up too. "I barely got out of the back before he drove away!" He shrugs miserably. "The Mazda's gone, Vince. With all our stuff in it."

"Describe him."

In spite of everything, Kendra's keen powers of observation come through. "Tall, kind of chunky, with a prominent nose and black hair . . ." I'm actually *proud* of her. How many eighteen-year-old girls could hold it together under these circumstances? ". . . and he was carrying a suitcase like yours." She blinks. "Vince, what happened to your suitcase?"

What are the odds? An entire airport full of potential getaway cars, and Uncle Bignose has to steal mine.

I take a deep breath. "Let me make a couple of calls."

I get in touch with Tommy on the first try.

He's incredulous. "He jacked *that* piece of crap? Man, Bignose must be slipping."

"Just get it back, will you?"

Luckily, Uncle Bignose has his cell phone on. To his credit, he gives Tommy excellent directions to the abandoned factory where he ditches the Mazda.

A taxi ride later, we're back on the road, a little wiser and three million poorer.

One other difference: Kendra is red-hot steaming mad.

"Vince, this is unacceptable. This time you can't just throw up your hands and say, 'Oh, my crazy family!' We were carjacked, and *you're* in cahoots with the carjacker! Tell me that's not what just happened!"

Needless to say, it's a very quiet drive to Denver, and on to Las Vegas the next day.

"It's been a pleasure," Alex beams as we unload the last of our stuff. He's been getting steadily happier ever since Kendra and I started fighting—cracking jokes, singing, and raving about the scenery.

"Go to hell," I mumble sourly.

He rolls his eyes at us. "You guys are such knuckleheads. If you were going to break up over something like this, it would have happened six months ago. You're in love. God knows why, but it's the real deal."

He hefts his final suitcase and disappears into the dorm, leaving the two of us standing there with stunned looks on our faces.

It's amazing. I mean, Alex is the ultimate unmarried marriage counselor. He's never had a second date, much less a girlfriend. But in this case, he's dead right. The Uncle Bignose thing—it wasn't exactly fun, but for us, it's old news. It'll take a lot more than that to derail the Vince and Kendra Express.

Her hand steals into mine, which is already en route to stealing into hers.

"How about that," she says mildly. "We went to high school with Dr. Phil, and we never even knew it."

I hold the car door open for her because chivalry isn't dead, even though my luggage probably is. "Three hundred miles to go."

That's romance for you. Three hundred good miles are more than enough to make up for a transcontinental bummer.

California, here we come.

CHAPTER TWO

KENDRA AND I HAVE always seen ourselves as a kind of modern-day Romeo and Juliet. But when I think about our storybook romance, Shakespeare isn't the author who comes to mind. Mario Puzo is a little closer to the mark.

Here's the thing: Dad's business is more than a nine-to-five job. Wiseguys call it The Life because it's exactly that. You can't turn it off for a couple of hours because your son's girlfriend is over for dinner for the first—and only—time.

Actually, I'm kind of amazed that Dad's willing to sign off on the plan at all. But at the Luca table, my mother is *capa di tutti capi*, the boss of bosses. She must have made her husband an offer he couldn't refuse.

It goes pretty well at first. Dad greets Kendra

politely, if a little quietly. Only I catch his meaningful gesture toward the chandelier, a popular location for one of her father's listening devices.

My mother serves her famous gnocchi—potato-pasta dumplings so dense, that each has its own gravitational field. They're great—Mom's a fantastic cook. But Kendra's petite, so she's stuffed in five minutes. It's a classic miscalculation in our dining room: she assumes that the soup, salad, antipasto, and the parade of dishes to follow are dinner. She doesn't realize that all this has been nothing more than batting practice, the warmup to some serious eating.

And then the meal is seasoned with a little dash of the vending machine business.

There's a pounding at the door, and in staggers Benny the Zit, who sometimes does odd jobs for Tommy. He looks like something out of *Dawn of the Dead*—covered from head to toe in blood, with a stainless-steel corkscrew buried in his neck up to the third spiral.

My father, who just turned sixty and claims to be slowing down, leaps out of his chair, charges across the foyer, and leaves his feet like an NFL linebacker. He hits Benny right between the numbers, driving him back outside. The door slams shut behind them.

"Old family friend," Mom tells Kendra confidentially. "Poor boy cut himself shaving."

From our front stoop comes an earsplitting scream as Dad yanks the corkscrew from Benny's flesh.

Mom has an explanation for this, too. "Owls. They're all over the neighborhood."

For the rest of the meal, we pretend to concentrate on our food, and not the howls of agony that come as my father, who includes amateur surgery on his list of talents, stitches up Benny the Zit in our not-very-sterile garage. Kendra hangs tough, but at one point, I look over, and she's gone so pale that she appears to have no lips.

She's still a little shaky when I drop her at home. "Is your house like that every night?"

"No," I deadpan. "Mom only makes gnocchi on special occasions." And we crack up laughing.

Mom hands down her judgment that night. "A beautiful girl—a lovely person. Don't bring her here no more. Do *her* a favor."

My mother acts clueless around Dad's business, playing obedient homemaker, but I'm not fooled. She's harder than the granite countertop she presides over. Where family is concerned, you don't want to cross Mom. You just might cut yourself shaving.

If the Lucas are a tough crowd for Kendra, her family is even worse for me. There's no question that her father hates my guts. Kendra insists it's a typical dad thing. You know—"No one will ever be good enough for my little girl."

Yeah, right. In Agent Bite-Me's dreams, one Luca goes to prison, and the other gets the electric chair. Guess which one is me.

It's a sticky set of emotions to sort through. I haven't done anything wrong, but Dad sure has. On the other hand, this is the man who carried me on his shoulders, who coached my Little League team, who's devoted to his kids without reservation. It would kill me to see him go to jail.

Add in Kendra, who loves this stranger who's dead set on bringing down my dad and shattering my family. It's a mess.

When I'm in the Bightly house, the walls seem to close in on me. It's enemy territory, and I feel it.

"This isn't Quantico, you know," Kendra reminds me. "I told you, my dad doesn't bring work home."

I never fully accept that. Like the time I catch sight of the notepad by the telephone in Kendra's kitchen. There, scrawled in a masculine hand, is: *Tuesday—2:45pm—JFK—Delta.*

I know a lot of the crews in the Luca organization make money hijacking the trucks that unload international cargo shipments at Kennedy airport. So when I see the note, I'm positive it's a tip-off about a heist.

The information haunts me. I know Dad isn't going to be personally involved in a truck robbery. But these things have a ripple effect. The connected guys rat out the made guys, the made guys rat out the captains, and the captains rat out their boss.

I sure can't warn Dad. That's the equivalent of giving him a spy inside the FBI. I mean, I love him, but I don't want to be his accomplice.

On Tuesday afternoon, I drive to the airport myself—not to the passenger terminals, but the cargo area. I'm not even sure what my plan is. If I recognize any of my father's people, I guess I'll just try to scare them off. Dad has promised not to let them involve me in anything illegal. So if I refuse to go away, they'll have no choice but to cancel the job.

For five long hours, I hang around the cargo area, navigating the cloverleaf of potholed roadway. I don't see anybody. I follow a few eighteen-wheelers as far as the expressway ramp, but nobody messes with them.

By the time I get home, I'm a wreck, pummeled by nerves, frustration, and boredom.

"Guess what?" Kendra tells me over the phone. "My grandmother's visiting us. We just got back from the airport."

Well, Granny didn't arrive in a cargo crate, that's for sure.

Okay, I'm being paranoid. But that doesn't necessarily mean everybody *isn't* out to get you. And I know I'm not crazy about the watch. It's a Rolex—my eighteenth-birthday present from my parents. Agent Bite-Me thinks it's hot. Every time we're together, he just stares at the thing, and I can tell he's sifting through recent robberies, trying to match it to some crime.

To be honest, I don't even blame him. Three quarters of the stuff in my house is swag—stolen merchandise. Rugs, furniture, lamps, appliances, electronics—it all fell off a truck somewhere. When we redid the kitchen, we hired a real contractor, but Dad brought in the tile and cabinets himself, and you know what that means. Even in our four-car garage, my beat-up old Mazda is the only member of the Luca fleet that anybody actually bought.

It starts eating at me: I've gone to such lengths to separate myself from the business. Am I wearing swag on my wrist? When I check the time, am I participating, in a small way, in my father's world?

I'll never get a straight answer out of Dad, so I go to work on Mom. I don't ask outright; I dance around the subject, posing a few pointed questions about the watch. Where was it purchased? Did Dad do the shopping? Was it a credit card or cash transaction? Did he send one of the uncles to pick it up?

She's an absolute clam. But a couple of days later, I find a piece of paper lying on my bed. The numbers are discreetly blacked out, but it's the store receipt for my birthday present.

I do two things: I fax it to the FBI's New York tip line, attention Agent Bightly. And I resolve never again to set foot inside Kendra's house when her dad is home. From that moment forward, I see the guy only during pickup and drop-off—with one exception.

Did you ever view an event with such total soul-shaking dread that the only way to put it out of your mind is by pretending it's never going to happen? That's how I feel about high school graduation.

On this day, for the first time ever, Anthony Luca and Agent Bite-Me will be in the same room together. Forget caps and gowns: I think the class of '04 had better rent flak jackets. There will be fireworks.

We try everything to keep them apart. I'm introducing my folks to kids I haven't spoken to since third grade. Kendra maneuvers her dad into conversation with the chemistry teacher, whose three-hundred-fifty-pound bulk blocks eighty percent of the sightlines in the gym.

But the law of averages is against us. In the end, the crush around the refreshment table is our downfall. For the sake of a couple of chocolate rugalach, Mr. and Mrs. Bightly find themselves face-to-face with Mr. and Mrs. Luca.

The silence is nothing short of apocalyptic. It occurs to me that the only other possible scenario for this meeting would be my father's trial.

God only knows where Kendra gets the nerve to perform the introductions, but she does it, albeit in a voice several octaves higher than usual.

"Mom, Dad, these are Vince's parents."

Just as I'm praying for someone to pull the fire alarm, my father extends his hand to the man who has been dogging him, spying on him, and bugging his house for years.

"Anthony Luca. How's it going? I feel like you know me."

Oh, how I love my dad right then. That one

remark defuses the situation long enough for the two adversaries to shake and get the hell out of there. I wish I could say that our families put aside their differences for this one occasion and we all go to dinner and have the time of our lives. But the truth is, our fathers hate each other more than they love us, and maybe that's not wrong. After all, they play in a league where the stakes are frighteningly high.

So you can forgive me a little cockiness when it comes to Kendra and me. We've been through the shredder, and we're still hot and heavy. I'm starting to believe our relationship can survive anything.

I don't know it yet, but my theory is about to be sorely tested.

CHAPTER THREE

PACIFIC PALISADES, California. Kendra and I are just working up to a very memorable goodbye when her roommate barges in.

Beth is a cute corn-fed girl from the Midwest somewhere. "The kind of town where the top circulating material in the library is *Guns & Ammo*," she informs us. "You're so lucky to be from a place that's more liberal-thinking."

True. Where I come from, nobody needs a magazine to teach you what to do with guns and ammo.

She seems a little disappointed to be rooming with someone who already has a steady boyfriend.

"Don't worry," Kendra assures her. "Vince and I aren't joined at the hip. We agreed to give each other the space to experience what college has to offer."

News to me.

Beth is a French horn player—a pretty good one, apparently, if she's talented enough to get into Burrell Music Academy. Kendra wants to be a singer, but it's her piano playing that got her ticket punched at BMA. She has a great voice, but it's untrained, and top musical conservatories would never accept somebody based on her karaoke stylings.

Pretty soon, there's a duet going on—Beth on the French horn, accompanied by Kendra on her electric keyboard. I say my farewells and retreat before they drag out the karaoke machine. I know when I'm a third wheel. Besides, I've got my own dorm to check into.

The University of Santa Monica is only a handful of miles down the curve of the coastline, but rush-hour traffic makes it a thirty-minute drive. I double that figure by getting lost.

Louis B. Mayer Hall doesn't look much like a college residence. It's actually an old mission-style church that the university converted into a dorm.

At least moving in won't be a major operation. Most of my stuff is being x-rayed and irradiated by the FBI. One confusing note: my confirmation says I'm in room 601, but Mayer Hall is only a four-story building. Turns out, I'm in the *bell tower*. I have to take the elevator to the fourth floor, and schlep up a dark claustrophobic staircase to my new home.

On the first landing sits a narrow footstool. A small tripod balances on the seat, supporting an amateur telescope, which is pointed deliberately out the narrow turret window at the apartment building across the street. I've not yet met my neighbors, of course. But I already know one of them is a peeping Tom.

I turn my key in the lock and step into 601. It's a typical dorm room, a little smaller than Kendra's, painted a drab beige. There are windows on three walls. To the north are the Santa Monica mountains. To the east, the vast city of Los Angeles. And to the west, as far as the eye can see, the blue Pacific.

I kind of understand how a lighthouse keeper must feel, suspended above the vistas at his post on the edge of the world. I chose Santa Monica because it was the film school as far from my father's business as I could get without actually falling off the continent. Looking out at this scene that could not be less like New York, the message fills me like a balloon: *You made it. You're here. You're free.*

I have to share this paradise with someone, of course. Although my roommate isn't here, his presence is obvious. Our space is exactly fifty-percent occupied—one made bed, one full dresser, one cluttered desk. The left side of the closet is jammed with clothes and shoes. Even half of the wall space is plastered with posters. The remaining portion of the room—mine—is as bare as the days when monks lived here.

It isn't much less empty after I move in. Until I can cash in that plane ticket, I'm down to a laptop, a video camera for TV production class, and a few hasty purchases—bed linens, shirts and pants in an Old Navy bag, and a few emergency toiletries.

I pick up my phone and dial Alex on his cell. Evidently, he's having no trouble finding things to do at UNLV, because I get his voice-mail message: "I don't have time to talk to you! I'm in Vegas, man!" There's a bloodcurdling scream that sounds something like "Pa-a-arty!" followed by a beep.

"It's me," I say. "Good to know you're keeping it low-key—"

The door opens, and a tanned, blond-haired kid, very MTV-looking, breezes in. He marches deliberately up to me, throws his arms wide, and invites me into a bear hug of greeting.

"Uh—gotta go." I get off the cell and try to downgrade the hug to a handshake. We end up with half embrace, half high five, all awkward.

He talks a mile a minute—the campus, the weather, the parties, the girls. An ad agency could scarcely do a better job selling this place. I don't catch many of the machine-gun details, except his name: Trey. Trey Sutter.

"Vince Luca," I introduce myself, adding, "I guess you moved in early."

"Oh, yeah, since ten o'clock this morning. You know, scoping out the scene." He frowns at my anemic collection of earthly possessions. "Traveling light?"

"Luggage problems. My suitcase is still in New York."

"You're from New York?" he crows. "How awesome is this? You hit the jackpot, *hombre*! Your roommate is the ultimate Angeleno—Beverly Hills, 90210, born and raised. It's not like Back East here. The town's not going to reach out and grab you by the throat. Don't get me wrong—this is a smokin' place, but you have to put in the effort. You've got to make the city work for you."

"Uh, thanks—"

"Let me hear you say it," he insists.

I swallow. "The city has to work for me."

"You have to *make* it work for you." He puts an arm around my shoulder. "Don't worry, man. I'll be with you every step of the way. This is going to be the best year of our—"

There's a polite knock at the door, and in steps a distinguished, middle-aged man in what my mother calls a sign-on-the-dotted-line suit. His head is capped by a frosted version of Trey's short yet somehow bushy hair.

Trey's smile vanishes, his shoulders slump, and his lips curl into a sneer. His arms cross in front of him in a pose that screams: *Defense!*

"I brought your alarm clock," Mr. Sutter says, placing a futuristic-looking travel beeper on the nightstand. "Mom thought it might be nice if you woke up for the occasional class."

A grunt is all the acknowledgment he gets from his son.

Mr. Sutter's piercing blue eyes fall on me. He looks somehow familiar, although I don't see how I could have met him. "Aren't you going to introduce me to your roommate?"

Apparently not, because Trey just stands there.

"I'm Vince," I say into the uncomfortable silence. "From New York."

"Bill Sutter." He grabs my hand and pumps it with gusto. "Easterner, huh? I love it there. In fact, I'm heading out this afternoon. Washington—my home away from home."

That's why I recognize the guy! Representative William Sutter. He's one of those hotshot congressmen who are always getting interviewed on TV. I've seen him on the news and the Sunday-morning talk shows.

"Pleased to meet you." And I am. I've never met a real congressman before. Dad's business doesn't attract a very sophisticated crowd. That's not to say they're all stupid. Anthony Luca is one of the sharpest people I know. But he's not educated and polished like Trey's father. There's talk about William Sutter running for *president* someday!

How much more different can two fathers be? Respected public servant—Mob boss. This is exactly why I came to California—to escape Dad's world. And I'll be living with a guy from a background that's the total opposite of mine. Perfect.

Representative Sutter consults his watch. "I've got a plane to catch. Good meeting you, Vince." He hugs Trey, who squirms out of his embrace. "Try opening a book every now and then," he advises. "We're proud of you, kid." He strides out.

Clearly, Trey doesn't relish being the son of a Washington bigwig. He should walk a mile in my shoes.

I do my best to smooth things over. "My first celebrity sighting."

"He's a jerk."

"Seems pretty nice to me."

"His whole life is a power trip," Trey says dismissively. "He'll do anything to get on TV. And when it's an election year, forget it. I have to be perfect to make him look good. It's like living in a fishbowl."

Try moving your bowels when your girlfriend's father has the house bugged.

"So, what does *your* old man do?" Trey inquires.

"He's in"—my face twists—"vending machines."

"You mean the ones that sell Coke?"

"And candy, potato chips"—I feel ridiculous, but I can't stop—"sometimes ChapStick . . ."

He's genuinely interested. "There's money in that kind of stuff?"

The racketeering part pays pretty well—if you don't get caught. Or whacked. "I've got issues with my family, just like you."

"Don't be too hard on your old man," he advises me. "If there's one thing I've learned from

Congressman Phony, it's that there's nothing wrong with an honest job."

I don't doubt he's right. But what would Anthony Luca know about an honest job?

As I settle in, stashing away my meager belongings, one thing becomes obvious: Trey Sutter's primary purpose in college is to attract as much attention as humanly possible.

Our door is always wide open so the blasting music can reach people in the stairwell and halls below. In the entryway to room 601, an enormous Union Jack hangs from ceiling to floor. At least ten people duck in to greet the two British students.

"Take it down," I plead for the umpteenth time. "Everybody thinks we're idiots."

"You're in California, *hombre*. You've got to make a statement."

"Yeah, but what statement?" I counter. "That we're from England?"

"The statement is that you're making a statement," he explains reasonably. "Nobody cares what you're making a statement *about*. Half the kids in this school have Einstein posters on their walls. If they're so smart, why aren't they at Harvard?"

At least we get to meet some of the locals, including our fellow monks in Mayer Hall's bell tower.

Perry, a junior, and his senior roommate, Calvin, are the denizens of 501, and the keepers of the telescope on the landing outside their room. Turns out, they're fans, not voyeurs. The spy setup is aimed at a luxury condo owned by none other than former Beatle Ringo Starr.

"Yeah?" I peer into the lens, but all I see is a window dressed with calico curtains. "You've seen him?"

"Never," Calvin admits.

"So how can you be sure he really lives there?" I ask.

"This is L.A.," Trey informs me. "Everybody knows the stars' secret hideaways. The problem is these guys have so many houses around the world that it's tough to nail them down in any one place."

Calvin asserts that if he doesn't catch a glimpse of Ringo before graduation, he intends to kill himself. Perry is in favor of this, since USM rules state that if your roommate commits suicide, you get an automatic 4.0 average. It's hard to know exactly how seriously to take these guys. They're obviously joking, yet there are no telltale smirks or snickers. They seem pretty passionate about the whole thing.

Upstairs in 701 live two sophomore girls, blond, blue-eyed twins Alita and Anthea. Everybody calls them Alitalia and Anorexia. Supposedly, there are two more sisters at home named Ariel and Allegra. Good thing they're still in high school, because we're running out of nicknames. The fastidious, preppy twins are the polar opposite of Calvin and Perry, who state with pride that they have never once cleaned their bathroom in more than two years of living together.

Next is 801, the penthouse, with the most coveted view in Mayer Hall. Mitch the Bean Counter lives up there with a film major named P. Richard Shapiro, who I haven't met yet. Nobody has, except Mitch.

"Yeah, P-Rick doesn't hang around here much," he tells us. "Not even to sleep."

"He's got a girlfriend, huh?" puts in Trey.

"Not unless she lives in the editing room. That's where he spends all his time."

"But classes haven't even started yet," I point out. "How could he be working on a film already?"

Mitch shoots me a meaningful look. "P-Rick's a serious artist. Just ask him. He'll tell you."

We meet a few kids from the lower floors, too,

but not many. The bell tower doesn't attract much passing traffic. Unless you know somebody in our little aerie, there's no reason to be on those stairs.

"The trogs don't like to come up here," Perry explains to me. "Too close to God."

"To close to Perry," Alitalia amends. "And that stench coming out of his room."

"She wants me, big-time," Perry concludes. "The insults—that's our courtship dance."

"Are you interested in her?" I probe.

His answer is a halfhearted shrug. "Not particularly, but we'll probably end up together. I could never date a trog."

"Except maybe one with no sense of smell," she adds.

This sounds as if Perry and Alitalia spend a lot of time together. The truth is, they barely speak to each other except through me. That seems to be part of the job in room 601—to act as an information conduit between 501 and 701. It's how you pay for the view.

Sounds like a fair deal to me.

"Well, we've met everybody except P-Rick." I yawn. "And I'll be seeing him around the film school. What say we take down the flag and—"

The sentence is not yet fully past my lips when

our Union Jack is pushed aside and in walks the most beautiful creature I've ever laid eyes on.

Willow. Even her name is awesome. How can any girl named Willow *not* be stunning? I wouldn't trade Kendra for anybody, but Willow is drop-dead gorgeous—model slim, with wavy dark hair. Very Halle Berry–like, but with pale eyes the color of lime-green translucent Legos.

Funny, too. She slips gracefully past the flag and bursts into a rousing chorus of "God Save the Queen."

"We're not British," I confess.

Trey flashes his most engaging grin. "What nationality do you want us to be?"

She matches him tooth for tooth. In her case, the finished product belongs on a magazine cover. "Got any thumbtacks?"

"I'm lucky I have a change of underwear," I complain. "Luggage limbo."

But Trey has stashed in his desk a poster-hanging workshop with enough hardware to cover every billboard on the Sunset Strip.

So there we are at the corkboard on the landing with the telescope, pinning up Xeroxed flyers advertising the Fall Fling Bash at the Lambda Chi fraternity Friday night.

"You know, we don't get a ton of pedestrians

through here," I point out. "And I don't think the locals are the frat-party type."

"That's bull," she scoffs. "There's a party animal inside all of us, struggling to find the nearest keg." She beams at Trey. "Right?"

I read my roommate like a book. Confucius never spoke such profound wisdom. Then again, Confucius probably didn't have the abs to carry off a pair of low-rise jeans, either.

"This is the best party week," Willow continues. "The frats all want to impress the new talent so they'll get the most action in spring rush."

Trey looks amused. "Those guys must be pretty happening if they've got you as their den mother."

She laughs. "I used to date the pledge chair. He graduated last year. But I still know everybody. And anyway, believe me, it's *the* place to be. You guys should check it out."

Trey and I exchange a meaningful glance. "Last year"—that means Willow's an upperclassman. I haven't been in college very long, but one thing that's pretty clear is that upperclassmen don't have much to do with freshmen. Especially upperclassmen *girls* with freshmen *guys*. Turns out, Willow is a senior. Senior girls are women. Freshman guys are still in utero.

When an older girl who looks like Willow tells you to check something out, you check it out, even if it's a convention of sewer rats. Trey wouldn't miss this party even if he had to crawl there over hot coals.

And what does he say to her? "Yeah, maybe. We'll try to stop by. We've got a lot of places to hit that night."

Only when she disappears down the stairs does he allow himself a dance of triumph.

"This city is working for us!"

Mission Number One is my clothes.

"I just bought clothes," I protest.

"You bought clothes for middle school. Now you need something you can be seen in."

Since I'm close to broke, we have to find a Continental Airlines office to cash in my ticket from the Uncle Bignose incident.

The good news is that Anthony Luca springs for first class, so I step out into the late afternoon sun with more than a thousand bucks in my hot little hand.

With the instincts of a homing pigeon, my roommate drags me to Venice Beach, a funky, slightly seedy neighborhood next door to Santa Monica. Picture Greenwich Village with better parking and beach volleyball. The stores range from Starbucks and a dry cleaners to a place called Protective Fashion that sells bulletproof vests designed to fit under haute couture. One lingerie shop displays articles of underwear so stringy and bizarre that I honestly can't wrap my mind around where on the human body they're supposed to go.

Some of the names are tongue-in-cheek, like the jeweler called Rox, or Vintage Collectibles, where all the "collectibles" are classic cars. A '57 Chevy, a Rolls Corniche, and a midcentury Mercedes that could have been Hitler's staff car grace the showroom window. There's an Aston Martin worthy of James Bond, and even a Delorean, its doors opening straight up, giving it the appearance of an alien spacecraft. But Trey stops in front of a Volkswagen bus from the nineteen-sixties, painted psychedelic colors.

"I worship this car."

I frown. "An old Volkswagen?"

"A *new* old Volkswagen," he corrects me. "It got locked away in a storage room back in the sixties, so it was never sold. The odometer has, like, thirty miles on it. Whoever buys this baby gets a brand-new car, an instant classic!"

"You?" I inquire.

He makes a face. "The only way for me to buy

this car would be to beg the old man for the money. As if."

I feel an affinity for him right then. Like Trey, I could have any car I wanted. I'd just have to ask my father. Although in my case, it would definitely be hot.

"You'd never get the emissions certified anyway," I tell him. "That exhaust system is older than some of our professors."

"I don't have to drive it." He barely takes his eyes off the bus's Day-Glo finish. "I'm happy just to stand here and bask in its greatness."

Funny. I know a lot of guys who are into cars. They can lecture you at length over the pros and cons of Lamborghinis over Ferraris. None of them would ever look twice at an old VW. Why would a high-society kid like Trey choose this oddball as his Holy Grail?

Maybe it's hooked into his attitude about his father. After all, the car evokes images of the sixties, hippies, free love, and protest marches. What could be more opposite to a buttoned-down Republican congressman?

Our real destination turns out to be a small surf-style boutique called Bad Shark. They sell exactly the same clothes as the stuff I bought at Old Navy. But they're triple the price, and here each item bears the Bad Shark logo, a caricature of a leering sea predator about to gobble up a mermaid of *Baywatch*-like proportions.

I buy half the store.

Trey helps me haul the bags out to the Mazda. "You're going to be the bomb," he assures me.

"I'm going to be a billboard for Bad Shark. I've even got the socks, for God's sake."

"And the shades." He reaches into the pocket of his open Hawaiian shirt and pulls out a pair of sleek steel-rimmed sunglasses with the ever-present Bad Shark on the temples. "To complete the effect."

I stare at him. "You didn't pay for those!"

"Sure I did."

"Show me the receipt."

He shrugs. "I didn't keep it. Come on, *hombre*, don't give me a hard time about getting my roommate a little 'welcome to L.A.' present."

I thank him, but I practically choke over it. I can't prove anything of course, but there's no way he paid for those sunglasses.

Like there isn't enough crime in my life already, my roommate is a kleptomaniac.

CHAPTER FOUR

I MEET P. RICHARD Shapiro at ten A.M. Friday morning in TV production class. I begin hating his guts promptly at 10:03. Yes, it's a snap judgment, but I'm as sure of it as I am that the sun will rise tomorrow. P-Rick brings out those kinds of emotions in people. He is, in every possible sense, a P-Rick.

Mr. Baumgartner, the professor, is reviewing the syllabus, going over simple stuff like which end of the camera to hold, and the intricacies of removing a lens cap. But when he asks, "Any questions?" P-Rick comes to life like a pop-up carnival target.

"Do you have any thoughts on the death of the musical as a genre on television?"

Rule number one: never ask Mr. Baumgartner if he has thoughts on something. He has thoughts on *everything*, and he's more than happy to share them. This being a film class, the wandering of my mind takes on script form.

INT. SEMINAR ROOM—DAY

Twenty-four FRESHMEN sit, bored out of their minds, listening to MR. BAUMGARTNER and P-RICK lament the downfall of the TV musical at a cost of thirty-five thousand dollars per year.

CLOSE-UP ON VINCE . . .

his red face darkening to purple.

CLOSER ON . . .

a thick bulging VEIN in his forehead. It begins to throb visibly as a distorted guitar riff builds to crescendo, undulating with the action of the whammy bar, until . . .

BOOM!

VINCE spontaneously combusts, raining viscera, bone fragments, and shreds of clothing on his fellow students. . . .

"Well, Rick," the teacher says finally, "perhaps that should be your project in this class—to breathe life into this art form."

"Yes," P-Rick deadpans. "I'm working on a script for a musical comedy based on the Bible story of the sacrifice of Isaac."

I laugh out loud. I mean, he has to be kidding, right?

P-Rick peers down the slope of his long straight nose at me. To say he regards me as if I were a kitchen cockroach doesn't do it justice. He looks at me like I'm the *second* cockroach he's noticed, proving that the first wasn't a random occurrence. This is an infestation.

The worst part is after class, Mr. B makes a point of getting the two of us together. "According to my info, you both live in Mayer Hall. Maybe you can partner up."

"I work alone," says P-Rick.

Thank God for that.

"But television is a *collaborative* medium," the professor protests. "No man is an island in this business. We need writers and actors and crew. People behind the cameras, between the head-phones—"

"But a shooting set is not a democracy," P-Rick argues. "The director has final say over every-thing, and there can only be one of those."

In other words, if I want to be this creep's peon, he'll allow me to hold up a spotlight or a mike boom while he runs the show. "Yeah, well, I've got a few ideas of my own I've been working on." It's an absolute lie, but I'm not going to sign on the dotted line to join Team Shapiro.

It's amicable enough, but there's a problem. We have to go home, and since our point of origin and destination are the same, we end up walking together.

It's pretty awkward. Not for P-Rick. He seems perfectly content to cross the campus and possibly circumnavigate the globe without a word of conversation. But it's driving me crazy. Maybe it's all those politeness lectures from Mom—*you don't turn your nose up at people*. Who knows, maybe I just need to prove to myself that I'm a better man than P-Rick. But whatever the reason, I say it.

"Have you thought about recruiting performers from Burrell Music Academy? My girlfriend goes there. She could probably hook you up with some people."

The great P. Richard Shapiro actually looks interested. "Thanks. There are plenty of great musicians in L.A., but most of them wouldn't appear in a student production. Even mine."

It's a normal human interaction—my first with P-Rick. I offer help; he expresses gratitude. I almost like him then.

"Great. I'll give you her number."

Me and my big mouth.

The power chords of Black Sabbath's "Iron Man" can be heard from the Pacific Ocean halfway to the 405 freeway. All the frats, apparently, have a signature song used to summon the faithful to fun and merriment. This tribute to Ozzie Osbourne in his adopted hometown is Lambda Chi's clarion call. There are a lot of frat houses on the street, but some regular people too. They should sue.

It's only a few blocks away, but naturally we drive. This is L.A., where if you can't burn fossil fuels doing it, it isn't worth doing. I have to park almost as far away as we live, but in the other direction. Fraternity Row is jumping, and the heavy-metal mantras of all those Greeks mingle together into a cacophony like the revving of badly lubricated jet engines.

Frat houses in movies are these giant old plantation-type mansions with fanlights over the doors. But Santa Monica is a crowded part of L.A., with long, narrow lots. Lambda Chi house is a two-story Tudor, smallish from the front, with most of the space in its depth.

You can feel the air move from the pounding bass as you enter the bunting-draped door. The windows are all open too. The whole structure, essentially, is being used as a speaker.

This isn't my first frat party. But even if I attend them regularly until I'm sixty-nine, I may never get used to them. They're fun, sort of. At least, a lot of the attendees seem to be having a good time. But they're also kind of like riots, full of frantic people going at fever pitch. Conversations have to be screamed because of the noise level. Moving through the crowd is an act of bulldozing. And even something simple, like dipping a chip, is accomplished with force, energy, intensity.

The drinking is a big part of it. Shiny kegs gleam brighter than the wild eyes of the revelers who are gathered around, awaiting their turn at the tap.

Trey, of course, is the first guy in line. In no time at all, he's got a beer in each hand, and one balanced on his head. This is a talent impressive enough to draw the attention of several of the Lambda Chi brothers.

"The old man used to make me balance a book on my head," he explains cheerfully. "God forbid his son should have bad posture on TV."

This leads to a conversation on who the old man is. Pretty soon Trey is the center of attention. The Lambda Chi's have hooked a congressman's son, and they're not going to let him get away. Nor is he going to let them let him get away.

"This is my roommate, Vince, from New York."

He may as well be talking about his pet rock. One of the brothers tries to show some interest. "What does your father do in New York, Vince?"

"Optometrist." I reserve the vending machine response for conditions under a hundred decibels.

One of the beers is for me. I take a sip, tipping the cold liquid against my lips, but not drinking much of it.

The brothers are gathered around Trey like Secret Service agents. He flashes me a thumbs-up, and mouths the words, "We're in."

But I'm already pushing my way through the gyrating bodies on the dance floor. I doubt Trey's new fans even notice I'm gone. I wonder if Trey does.

I duck out onto the back porch in search of breathable air. All frat parties smell alike too—a mixture of tobacco smoke, sweat, cheap perfume, and spilled beer. I must have contributed to the spillage myself. My drink is half empty, and I haven't swallowed more than an eye-dropperful.

I empty the rest of the cup into a potted rubber-tree plant. Hey, I'm in L.A. I have a dorm room with a million-dollar view. Nobody's keeping tabs on me—not the most powerful wiseguy on Long Island, or worse, Mom. I can stay out all night, not wash my hands after going to the bathroom, and inject Liquid Plumber directly into a vein in my neck. True, I won't do these things, but the point is I *can*. I exist in a universe of infinite possibility. And I'm not going to waste my time sardine-packed in a throng of phonies.

How is it that a shared experience of idiocy, civil disobedience, and alcoholism turns people into brothers? Can it be the Greek letters nailed above the door of the house they live in?

The walls inside are festooned with hundreds of pictures of current and former Lambda Chi's. Special attention is given to the ones who have become "celebrities," like soap-opera regulars, and the guy who invented boil-in-the-bag rice. Even out here in the backyard there's a stone bench dedicated to the memory of some late brother who was Herbert Hoover's undersecretary of the navy. If my roommate wants in on this environment, he can have it. Let him steal sunglasses for the pledge committee.

I wander back into the party, determined to find Trey to tell him I'm bored, and I'm going home. Instead, he finds me.

"Jeez, Vince, the brothers are pissed at you! What'd you do that for?"

I'm in the dark. "Do what?"

"Skip says you dumped a beer on Stedman!"

"I didn't!" I defend myself.

"He saw you!" he accuses.

"Honest—I poured it out on a tree in the back-yard!"

"That's Stedman!" he hisses. "He's been out there for fifty years! That rubber-tree plant was a gift to the house from President Eisenhower!"

I'm disgusted. "They've got a plaque on every toilet seat and saltshaker, telling some story about the rich history of Lambda Chi! You'd think they'd at least stick a 'No Dumping' sign on their pet plant!"

Trey puts his arm around my shoulders. "Listen, *hombre*, having Congressman Hard-Ass for a father is no picnic. But every now and then there's a fringe benefit, and this is one. They love me; and they'll love you too—*if* you play the game."

"Come on, Trey," I argue. "Do we really need these people? What's so great about this place?"

And then, just when it looks as if I've got him thinking, the answer to that question drapes itself around both our necks.

"Guys—you came!"

It's Willow Danziger's navel. At least, that's the part I can't stop staring at.

"You didn't steer us wrong," Trey raves. "This is Party Central."

It plays very well with Willow. She takes his hands, places them on her bare sculpted waist, and backs him onto the dance floor. Needless to say, he goes where he's pushed. Any man with a pulse would do the same thing.

I'm jealous, no question about it. But mostly, watching them makes me miss Kendra. Okay, it's only been a few days, but that's probably our longest separation in almost a year of dating. All at once I remember why this frat party touches such a nerve in me. Kendra and I kissed for the very first time at an NYU frat party. I got head lice from her, but it was a small price to pay.

All this—the earsplitting music, the crush of frenzied undergrads, the beer-soaked humidity— for me, it's a subconscious game of *Blue's Clues*. And the answer is Kendra.

I feel no guilt about running out on Trey. He's in good hands. And anyway, his walk home is shorter than his walk to the car.

The place is now so crowded that it takes me a good fifteen minutes to make it to the front door. And as I head down the block, latecomers are streaming past me. I barely notice them. My mind is focused on simple concepts: car; north; Kendra.

The roads are congested. Every missed light seems unbearable, as if I'm being held back from my destiny. I can see her dorm, but I can't get there. *Come on.*

I hear her voice as soon as I get off the elevator. She sings a full octave lower than she speaks—a deep, throaty contralto that's flat-out sexy. I stand outside her partly open door, a goofy grin all over my face.

"Kendra—" I say when she's finished.

Startled, she hurries out into the hall. I catch a brief glimpse of someone else in there as she pulls the door shut.

"Vince, what are you doing here?"

I move to kiss her, but she leans away from me.

"I had to see you," I confess. "I was at a frat party, and it reminded me of that night at NYU."

She looks uncomfortable. "What did you need to see me about?"

"I don't know. To talk about it, I guess. It's been a weird night—" It hits me. "You're blowing me off?"

"I'm kind of in the middle of something," she tries to explain.

Now I'm suspicious. I push into the room to see none other than P. Richard Shapiro sitting on the edge of my girlfriend's bed, fiddling with a pocketsize digital audio recorder.

He beams at me. "I can't tell you how grateful I am. Kendra's going to play the lead in *Burnt Offering*."

She's actually blushing.

"I didn't think *you'd* be able to do it," I mumble to her, a little resentfully. "You know, no free time, too much work—"

"This *is* my work," she reasons. "How can I pass up a chance to perform for one of America's most promising young directors?"

Promising? What's he promising my girlfriend?

P-Rick snorts. "Our department is a joke. Mr. Baumgartner couldn't even begin to imagine what I have in mind for this project."

I turn beseeching eyes on Kendra. But she's gazing at him worshipfully, totally snowed.

There's nothing left to do but get out of the way of great art.

She kisses me good-bye, but it feels rushed. Her lips are there, but her heart is back in P-Rick's musical.

I swallow hard. "Congratulations on getting the lead. What's the part, anyway?"

"Sarah." She beams. "Mother of the Hebrew nation."

Well, okay. But if P-Rick is casting himself as Abraham, there had better not be a big make-out scene.

CHAPTER FIVE

A TELEPHONE UPDATE from Alex at UNLV.

"School's awesome, Vince! Vegas is the ultimate town! Your pal Frankie—he's the greatest guy in the world!"

"Aw, Alex!" I groan. "I warned you about getting mixed up with anybody you meet through my family. Remember, this guy is *Tommy's* friend. God only knows what he's involved in."

"I know exactly what he's involved in," Alex raves. "He's a talent scout for the casinos. He knows every chorus girl, dancer, and hot chick in town! I've been waiting my whole life for a friend like this! Instead, I had to grow up with *you*."

I laugh, but I sound a cautious note. "Watch yourself. You don't know these Mob guys like I do."

He's in denial. "I just told you. He's not a Mob

guy. He's a businessman, a connoisseur of beauty and talent."

"It gets out of hand really fast with these people," I warn. "One minute you're blood brothers, and the next, he's gone, and the cops are looking for *you*."

"It's not like that with Frankie and me," he swears. "We're real friends. We help each other out. Like, he'll be bunking with me for a few days while his apartment gets painted."

"Some businessman," I retort. "Sleeping on the floor of a freshman dorm room. He's a regular impresario. Hollywood must be beating down his door."

"Hey, man, times are tough," Alex protests. "You can't fault the guy for trying to save a few bucks. Not everybody's Dad is the Godfather, you know."

Very true, I think as I hang up. Some dads are respected public servants, powerful congressmen who are quoted in newspapers and interviewed on CNN—and their sons still hate their guts.

"Look at this!" snarls Trey in disgust, unzipping the garment bag that's just been delivered by a Rodeo Drive designer shop. "Compliments of the old man! Like I'd wear it!"

I'm impressed. "That's a Hugo Boss suit! It

probably cost fifteen hundred bucks!" Not that I'm a fashion expert, but I do know a lot about Hugo Boss suits. I came home from school one afternoon and found two hundred and fifty of them, in various sizes, hanging off the water pipes in our basement. Dad told me Hugo Boss had had a clearance sale. But when the *New York Times* wrote it up, they didn't use the word *sale*. They called it a warehouse robbery.

"It's a great present. Is it your birthday or something?"

"That's no present," Trey scoffs. "He's probably got some big family-man photo op coming up, and he thinks I'll look more respectable in this rag."

I laugh. "Maybe you can get them to sew a Bad Shark on the lapel. Then you can wear it."

"Oh, I'll wear it, all right," he laughs. He takes this *GQ* garment, wads up the jacket and pants, and crams them into an empty computer box. Then he crushes the lid into place with his Shakespeare textbook—the complete works. By the time he puts on that suit, it's going to resemble a used Kleenex. It's almost painful to watch, like someone deliberately putting a key scratch on a really nice car.

"What if he doesn't have an ulterior motive?" I suggest. "What if it's just a gift?"

He smiles cynically. "My father doesn't give

gifts. If it comes from him, it's either bribery or extortion. You don't know how lucky you are, Vince, to be part of a normal family."

Oh, sure. What would my family know about bribery and extortion?

I find it pretty hard to feel sorry for Trey Sutter, because he's been dating Willow for the better part of a week. I can tell by his smile, his swagger, and the fact that he won't shut up about it for a nanosecond.

I can also tell by the tooth marks on his neck. Obviously, Willow is part vampire, because every time Trey gets together with her, he comes back with the same perforated crescent of tiny welts in the soft fuzz behind his ears.

I first ask him about it the morning after the Lambda Chi party.

"I don't kiss and tell," he says primly, and then proceeds to describe his night in such detail that I have to beg him to shut up.

"Oh, come on," he complains. "What's the point of fooling around with a girl like Willow if you can't brag about it it? I've got to get a picture of her." He looks thoughtful. "Better make it digital, so I can e-mail it to people."

I shouldn't be jealous. I've got the greatest girlfriend in the world. But between Kendra's freshman schedule at BMA and her starring role in *Burnt Offering*, the two of us haven't been alone together since our arrival in L.A. Meanwhile, my roommate is dating the world's ultimate adolescent fantasy. To be honest, it's a little painful.

And not just because Willow's great looking. If there's a leisure-time activity that girl isn't willing to try, I haven't heard of it. She surfs. She mountain bikes. She Jet-Skis.

She's up for anything. When Trey wants to try paintball at the arcade at the pier, she's psyched. I watch them through a chain-link fence. This has become a metaphor for my love life—observing Trey and Willow, on the outside looking in.

But Willow doesn't need to be entertained. If you tell her that you want to waste an entire day watching football and eating junk food, she's game for that too. She cheers every bone-cracking hit while taking bites of a greasy bacon cheeseburger that Kendra would quarantine behind concertina wire.

Willow doesn't even mind hanging out in Perry's room, and I know *guys* who can barely stand the noxious cocktail of foot odor and entombed flatulence in there. And she's just as anxious as the rest of us to catch a Ringo sighting.

"She's a keeper," Perry decides. "You know, for

a trog." It's the first nice thing I ever hear him say about someone who doesn't live in the bell tower.

I mean, Kendra's terrific, but could she recite *Monty Python and the Holy Grail* in its entirety while eating nachos made with habanero-pepper salsa, her own recipe? Trey's hit a real grand slam—a girlfriend and best buddy, all rolled into one. He's dating the ideal woman; I'm dating the human scheduling conflict.

On top of it all, I'm officially banned from Lambda Chi House. Stedman, the rubber tree plant from President Eisenhower, is going brown at the leaf tips, and my half beer is the prime suspect. The pledge chair himself passed the word along to Trey. Brotherhood in Lambda Chi is his for the asking, but his roommate, the optometrist's son from New York, is persona non grata.

"Don't worry, Vince," Trey says, trying to soothe me. "If Stedman pulls through, I'm sure I can convince them to give you another chance. It's a long time till spring rush. It'll all blow over."

I set aside the fact that I wouldn't join those idiots if they paid me, and sink into a depression at being rejected by the whole world.

"This city isn't working for me," I tell him plaintively.

I'm grateful for schoolwork—anything to keep

my mind off my social life. Not that college courses require much class time, especially for film majors. We're supposed to be out there, writing scripts and shooting video.

But I'm spending most of my time at my job at the foreign student office of the film school. I don't really have to work. But I want my spending money, at least, to be untainted by organized crime, even if my tuition comes from Dad's ill-gotten gains.

My job is to try to calm hysterical foreign students who are terrified of a) flunking out, b) having their funding cut, or c) being deported. They speak very little English, and I speak nothing but. Our only common language is hand gestures. I have no idea why I was hired. Maybe I was the only applicant stupid enough to sign on the dotted line.

It's the second week of school, and I've just spent the better part of two hours with a guy named Sato from Japan, filling out forms to get his visa reinstated. He's accompanied by Olaf, who calls himself Scooby—*Scooby-Doo* is apparently a cult classic in Oslo these days. I still haven't seen Scooby's face. He has a Palmcorder permanently glued to his eye socket. The Norwegian is determined to turn his entire college experience into the ultimate reality show, and allegedly spends all his waking moments videotaping "life." That includes Sato's immigration problems, me blowing my nose, and Carl, my boss, leaning in to tell me that my last appointment of the day is getting antsy.

"We're just about done here," I promise with a pointed look at the camera.

"You don't want to keep this guy waiting," Carl says ominously and disappears.

When I finally get rid of them, rough hands grab me from behind, covering my eyes. I struggle, but my attacker is too powerful. My heart is pounding—but sinking too as I realize I don't stand a chance against this trained professional. My father is tough, but so are his enemies, if this is one of them.

"What do you want?" I rasp, flailing with immobilized arms.

"Take a whiff!" orders a gruff voice that I can't quite place.

If I didn't know better, I'd swear I'm in the presence of my mother's famous five-cheese baked ziti. What a weird thought for a moment like this.

With a burst of strength, I twist free. Snatching a stapler up off the desk, I wheel, ready to bring the weapon down on my assailant's head.

And I'm staring at a teddy bear smile on the body of a grizzly.

"Tommy!" I howl. "What are you doing here?"

He holds up a Tupperware dish, proving that my Luca nose never betrays me. "Mom thinks they got no food in L.A."

"Mom's A-one right!" I exclaim. "For sure our cafeteria doesn't have any. Let's get this to a microwave!"

Luckily, we've got one back at the dorm, thanks to Trey.

My brother looks around the small room with distaste. "God, Vince, this place is a hole! What's Dad paying for it? Thirty-five large? College is a scam!"

I'm already shoveling ziti with a plastic fork, ignoring the burning of my tongue. "You come here for an education," I mumble, "not a five-star hotel."

"Yeah, sure, okay," he agrees. "Where do *I* sleep?"

"The floor, I guess. We'll pile up some blankets. And I think Trey has a sleeping bag. It's only for a couple of nights, right?"

He gets that look on his face, the one that says, *It's a little more complicated than that.*

"The thing is, Vince, I got into a bit of a beef back home. You know that guy Shlomo from Ozone Park? I kind of took a whiz on his brand-new

Hummer, because what's he going to do about it, right? Turns out he's hooked up with some of the Gambinos, and you know how they are about their cars. So Dad says, 'Go make sure your brother's studying hard.'"

I take a deep breath. "So you're here—"

"From now on," he finishes my sentence. "At least until Dad gives the all-clear."

Just when you think you're moving away from home, home comes and moves in with you. "That must have been some whiz," I remark. "Were the windows open?"

He laughs. "I missed you, kid."

"But, seriously," I continue, "you can't stay forever. We're all college students here. You're a"—I pause—"businessman."

"I'm off the clock in L.A. Scout's honor." He salutes incorrectly. Tommy was kicked out of Cubs for fencing counterfeit merit badges, so his scouting skills aren't up to par. He motions me closer. "Can you keep a secret, Vince?"

"What's up?" I ask.

"I'm thinking of calling it quits. Getting out of The Life."

"You're kidding! I mean . . ." Even though I'm Anthony Luca's son, I'm in the dark about a lot of the inner workings of his organization. I get my info the same way everybody else does—from Mafia movies. "Will they let you? Didn't you swear some kind of oath?"

"I'm always a member," he explains, "but I just start doing other things to make a buck. It helps that Dad runs the show."

I'm skeptical. "What 'other things'?"

"That's what I'm here to find out. Nobody knows me in California. I got no connections. I'm free." He frowns at me. "Don't look so suspicious. You're the one who's always ragging on Dad's business. You should be happy about this."

It's true. Ever since I was old enough to figure out that the vending machine business isn't really about vending machines, I've been bugging Dad and Tommy to go straight. Our father's a lost cause. But Tommy . . .

"That's—great news," I manage. "It's just—"

"You don't think I can make it stick," he finishes.

And that's exactly what I think. The last thing Tommy was immersed in before the Mob was amniotic fluid. Growing up, all the guys he admired were either made or connected. He couldn't wait to quit school and join Dad's thing. He's never kept regular hours, never cashed a paycheck, never paid taxes. He thinks working means hanging around some sleazy bar with a bunch of dirtbags, waiting for the next score.

They don't call it The Life because it's a weekend hobby.

I'm a little worried about how Trey will react to his surprise roommate. After all, the Sutters are high society, and Tommy may as well have THUG tattooed on his forehead. But it turns out to be no sweat. To Trey, having some large transient sleeping on your floor is part of the quintessential college experience. He takes to Tommy instantly, even presenting him with an air mattress to go under his sleeping bag.

It's funny: Tommy, who can be as dense as titanium sometimes, instantly figures out Trey. "Nice of him to do that. He ripped it off, you know."

I nod sadly. "I think Trey's got a knack for the five-finger discount. How could you tell?"

He shrugs. "Brand new, no bag, no bill. These Wonder Breads—they're not so different from us. Only, we do it for a living; for them it's like racquetball."

"What happened to going straight?"

"Civilians don't steal? Stock trader: he buys low, he sells high. You think the cash he makes comes out of thin air? Somebody used to own it."

"But it isn't against the law," I point out.

"How's Dad any different? He's an investor. He puts his money on the street and he gets it back with interest."

Yes, at two points a week. Or the kneecaps of the poor sap who can't pay. "Not a word to Trey about Dad's investing style. Nobody here has a clue about that."

He bristles. "What are you, ashamed of us?"

"Yeah! And starting now, you should be too."

Tommy is completely unimpressed by my breathtaking view of the ocean, mountains, and urban sprawl. "Big deal—water, dirt, and houses. Weird place, L.A. Everybody's always talking about the city. Where is it?"

I try to explain. "It's more spread out than New York."

He snorts. "Back home, you want to go to the city, you point your hood ornament at the tallest building and step on the gas. Here, you drive and drive. You never know you got there, except some pinhead in a bowtie valet-parks your car."

My brother thinks it's blasphemy to turn a church into a dorm. But he practically breaks his neck to get his eye to the lens of the telescope to behold whatever X-rated image he assumes the instrument is pointed at. You should see the look on his face when Calvin explains about the search for the elusive Ringo.

"What the hell is a ringo?"

"Ringo Starr, the Beatle!"

"Hey, man, I'm just a normal guy, not some bug expert."

Add 1960s rock bands to the list of categories Tommy should avoid if he ever goes on *Jeopardy*.

One aspect of the view that has Tommy's whole-hearted endorsement is Willow Danziger. His eyes practically pop out of his head when he meets her. And I'm surprised to see that she checks him out pretty well too. Tommy's no male model. But Kendra always said that there was something "primitive" about him, and it never came across as a negative comment.

There's a Jackie Chan movie on TV, and pretty soon he, Trey, and Willow are embroiled in an argument over whether martial arts guys are as tough as heavyweight boxers. Two minutes later, I step out of the bathroom to see my brother in the process of taking a punch at her. Before I can even cry out, Willow sidesteps the blow, snatches his arm, and hurls Tommy's considerable bulk over her lowered shoulder. If my bed isn't there to break the fall, I swear he'd go straight through the floor.

"I haven't seen a chick who could do that since

Iron Maria from Bensonhurst," he marvels, after Trey and Willow head out to Lambda Chi for some frat thing. "And she had a face like the back end of a garbage truck." He slaps me on the back of the head. "Why can't you get a girlfriend like that instead of wasting your life on Jane Edgar Hoover?"

I drop my eyes. "You'll be pleased to know that Kendra and I have barely seen each other since coming out here."

He tries with very little success to conceal his joy. "Gee, that's too bad, Vince. I really liked her."

"We didn't break up," I assure him. "We're just both really busy." Except me, of course.

"Don't be so sure, kid. Relationships drop like flies in this kind of place. You could be on the market any minute. It should be you hanging around that frat, not Trey."

"If you must know," I retort, "I don't hang around that frat because they as good as told me to get lost."

"What?" He jumps to his feet. "Why?"

I have no stomach to go through the whole Stedman story. "For various reasons," I mutter, "including the fact that Trey's Dad's a congressman, and mine's an optometrist."

He doesn't hear me. He's on one of his rants.

"We Lucas are as good as anybody! Our grandfather fought in World War Two!"

"Yeah, for Mussolini."

"It still counts," he argues. "These frat boys need a lesson in respect."

My heart leaps into my throat, because I know how dangerous my brother can be. Tommy comes across as amusing sometimes, like a gentle giant. But the truth is there's nothing gentle about him. When he teaches a lesson, spleens get ruptured. I don't have any proof, and neither, thank God, does Kendra's father. But the fact is you don't get as high up as Tommy in a Mob family without having committed a murder. That's how it is with the Lucas. We're like a quirky sitcom until a sudden burst of violence underscores just how unfunny we really are.

"Tommy, you've got to promise me—don't go near that frat house. I'm not the frat type. Even if they begged me to join, I'd say no. This is a non-thing."

He looks totally innocent. "Sure, Vince. When have you ever known me to mix in?"

CHAPTER SIX

INT. DINGY CAFÉ—DAY

Bright sunlight streams into the dark
room. GABRIELLA sits down at the bar. She
lights a cigarette with a practiced
motion. Tendrils of smoke curl around her
head like a halo.

                    BARTENDER
          What'll it be?

                    GABRIELLA
          I drink to forget my life of pain.
          Pour me something strong so I can
          take my misery and put it in my
          behind.

          "Cut!" I bark as Tommy brays a guffaw in
my ear.

I run up to "Gabriella," actually, Zora, one of my foreign students—from Slovakia. I slap at the script. "You're supposed to say, 'put it all behind me,' not 'put it in my behind'!"

She opens wide eyes. "This is the same thing, no?"

"No!"

My lighting guys are laughing too, and the shadows shake bizarrely as the spotlights tremble atop their booms.

"Okay," I begin, "let's try it again—"

But it's no use. The extras are giggling at their tables. They're also foreign students, so jovial conversations bubble up in several different languages. Even Olaf/Scooby has lowered his Palmcorder to join the mirth.

My set has dissolved into chaos. It's the worst thing that can happen to a film student. Mr. B warned us about this. The hardest part of being a director, he says, isn't the story or the cinematography. It's people skills. If you can't get your actors and crew to do what you want them to, you're toast. More than anything else, you have to be in *control*.

"Quiet on the set," I order. Louder: *"Quiet!"*

Forget it. This a party, and I'm the sole pooper, a failed pooper at that. The small café resounds with merriment. Rahim, the stoic Iranian student I've cast as the bartender, can no longer keep a straight face. Even Zora is enjoying a laugh at her own expense. Somewhere across town, P. Richard Shapiro is running a well-oiled machine, with my own girlfriend singing on his command—while I flail and flounder like a beached octopus.

I catch some bored sympathy from the bar manager. The university has a deal with the café to make the place available for student projects during off hours. He's seen all this before, a fledgling director unable to manage his own shoot.

"Attention, everybody—"

The panic that wells up inside me goes far beyond flunking this particular assignment. I'm not a natural leader. I stink at this and I have to consider the possibility that I may never get any better. The possibility, essentially, that I'm wasting my time and a whole lot of my family's money being in film school in the first place.

"*YO!*" barks Tommy.

It's only a single syllable, but instant silence falls. My brother looks threateningly around the room. "The director's talking here." He nods at me. "Take it away, Vince."

I have the undivided attention of the room.

"Uh—thanks." Obviously, Tommy has no control problems. He's like Spielberg with brass knuckles. I wonder if any real filmmakers have ever considered hiring a New York mobster to hang around the set, keeping order. A lot fewer movies would go over budget.

Zora does better with her dialogue on the next couple of takes, but there's a new problem. We're running late, and Rahim has a class. He's the only one of my foreign students who can play the bartender, since he speaks English without an accent.

Tommy weighs in on that issue too. "Where do you think you're going, dogface?"

I quickly intercede on the Iranian's behalf. "The guy's come eight thousand miles to get an education, not to star in my video."

So Rahim is off the hook. He rushes out the door with a nervous glance over his shoulder. The question remains: who will play the bartender?

"I'll have to do it," Tommy says finally.

"You want to act?"

"What's to act? You say the words and pretend like it isn't fake, right?"

It isn't his theory of drama that blows me away. It's the fact that he's willing to be filmed in the first place. In the vending machine business, they use a slightly different term for videotape: evidence.

We had a pool party once, and Uncle Exit's wife made the mistake of bringing her camcorder. Dad stood in the bathroom and personally oversaw the flushing of every single millimeter of that tape. Uncle Exit and Aunt Palma were divorced within six months.

To a wiseguy, appearing on camera is like elective surgery: you'll probably be okay, but why take the risk?

It hits me: if Tommy wants to act in my project, maybe, just maybe, he's serious about going straight.

Eagerly, I hand over Rahim's copy of the script.

His lips move as he reads it. "I can't say this."

"Why not?"

"Anybody I know talked like this, I'd put him out of his misery."

I try to explain. "The bartender is a sensitive person. He's used to customers coming and telling him their problems."

He has a suggestion. "How about I say the same thing in my own words?"

I decide to give it a try. After all, even the greatest directors take advice from their actors. I take my place behind the camera tripod and call, "Action."

In my original script, the bartender asks

Gabriella to tell him a little about herself so he'll be in a better position to help her with her situation. Here's how it translates to Tommyspeak: "Listen, sister, I ain't your mother and I ain't your shrink. Why don't you give the world a break and stuff a sock in it?"

In the stunned silence that follows, Tommy grabs Zora by the back of the collar, pulls her close, and kisses her.

Needless to say, this isn't in the script. But I'm so dumbfounded that I can't seem to come up with the word *cut*. Zora goes rigid for a second, but then she starts kissing him back. It's like looking in somebody's window. I feel that *I'm* the intruder here. I'm definitely not the director.

And then—a muffled sound, suspiciously like *Hey!* and Zora is staggering back from him, screaming bloody murder.

Then I understand why. Sticking out of his belt is the butt of a pistol.

Everybody sees it, and there are a lot of *Heys!*, including a loud pointed one from the bar manager.

I'm so used to covering up for my family that the lie springs fully formed to my lips. "Tommy, I told you to take that back to the props department."

It convinces the foreign students, but the manager isn't fooled. "I run a nice quiet place," he announces firmly. "I don't need this kind of aggravation. Don't come back to film; don't come back to drink; just don't come back."

Lucky for me, the syllabus lists next week's lecture as "Scouting Out Locations."

I need a new script, preferably something that takes place in a dorm room. I have one of those, and no one can kick me out of it, even if my brother hides a Sherman tank in his pants.

Unfortunately, everybody has the same idea. That's film school—sitting in a dark room, watching two dozen three-minute melodramas, all set in dorm rooms. If you want to do anything original, your dorm has to be located on Mars.

It takes a lot of the glamour out of the movie business.

I'm also in three other classes—Film History, Freshman Composition, and Probability, which fulfills my math requirement.

The Probability course was invented by the professor, Mr. Lai, a cured compulsive gambler who now lectures on the odds, percentages, and averages of blackjack, craps, roulette, baccarat, and poker. I think that's how he stays on the wagon, by running simulated casino games and crafting long formulas representing your chance of drawing to an inside straight. It would be kind of laughable, except that stuff is *hard*! I took it because it was going to be a cinch course. I don't even own a deck of cards!

My final two credits this semester come from my work-study job with the foreign students. It's kind of ironic. They pay me for the job, but charge me for the credits. I'm starting to understand what Dad and the uncles mean when they talk about finding an angle.

I don't see how answering the office phone is going to make me the next Cecil B. DeMille, but I do other things too. People pour out their hearts to me in languages I can't even identify, and I empathize. I help them fill out insurance forms and credit card applications. And I solve problems. I'm the one who explains to Paolo that when he asks the butcher for "chopped cattle," what he really wants is hamburger.

I'm usually pretty tired by the time I stagger home from work. So it takes a moment to register when a female voice calls, "Check out the guy with the cute butt!"

I turn to see Willow waving at me from behind the wheel of a lavender Mini Cooper, with Trey beside her in the passenger seat.

"Whoa, nice pecs, too! This one's a stud!"

Now I know she's full of it. I don't have *any* pecs, much less nice ones. That's Willow's new thing. She pretends to be hot for my bod so I won't be jealous of the fact that she really *is* hot for Trey's.

I tried to use reverse psychology once. She was wearing a miniskirt, so I whistled and said, "Hot legs." It backfired. Instead of getting shy, she pranced around the room, causing her hem to billow in a perfect imitation of that old movie scene of Marilyn Monroe on the subway grating. Let me tell you, the original had much less effect on me when we screened it in film history class. In our dorm room, the effort of averting and refocusing my eyes made me nauseous.

"What's wrong, Vince?" Trey asked that day. "You look seasick."

So I'm not exactly thrilled to see them. It's not that I resent Trey for having a girlfriend. But when Trey's happy, he's just so much happier than everybody else, with a face-splitting dimpled grin, and enough energy to lift the power grid out of brownout. I'd swear the guy is bipolar, except I haven't seen much of the down side. Maybe when his dad's around, which has only happened once.

Anyway, Willow is so much the girlfriend of

every freshman's dreams, especially for a guy like Trey, who worships an ideal of what the college experience is supposed to be. And it definitely includes a half-moon hickey on the back of your neck. No wonder Trey's psyched. It isn't his fault that his girlfriend is up for anything, and my girlfriend is up for nothing except P-Rick's video.

They squeal into a parking space, and I catch a glimpse of the third occupant of the car. It's Paul Waghorn, the president of Lambda Chi. He leaps out of the backseat, nearly crushing Willow into the steering wheel. I endure a slap on the shoulder so hard that, if I had false teeth, they'd be on the sidewalk.

It's an awkward encounter, one I've been dreading. "Listen, man," I say contritely, "I'm sorry about Stedman. Who knew that a fifty-year-old plant could die from only half a cup of beer?"

"Stedman?" he scoffs. "Who cares about that old stinkweed? The strength of a fraternity is in its people."

"Well, you lucked out getting Trey," I tell him. "He's real quality." And the fact that his dad's a congressman can't hurt either. Maybe he'll be president one day, and give them another rubber-tree plant.

But that's not what Waghorn has in mind.

"Yeah, sure. Trey's great. But *you*, Vince. You're pledging too, right?"

Understanding is as instant as it is jarring. How did I go from Stedman-killing public enemy number one to Most Valuable Pledge? Well, let's just say it started the moment Tommy found out about the frat not wanting me. Retired or not, I *know* he went over there and put the screws to everybody.

I turn to Trey. "Hey—" He and Willow are making out behind the steering wheel. It's pretty intense, but I'm in no mood to respect their privacy. "Trey, have you seen my brother hanging around the frat house?"

He never even looks up. The answer comes from Waghorn, who has gone a little pale, and is not quite so jaunty as usual. "Nice guy, your brother. Really—nice."

I take pity. "Listen, Tommy's a big talker. Don't worry about him. And don't worry about me either. I'm not going to pledge."

He goes to pieces. "You *have* to!" Then, recovering, "I mean, all the brothers want you to! You're at the top of our list!"

I sigh. "Look, nobody rushes till the spring, right? We don't have to decide anything now."

"But we're sure about you, Vince," he swears earnestly. "Our Webmaster has even set up your e-mail address on our site. You're crazyvince@lambdachi.org."

"Why crazy?"

He looks scared. "It's nothing personal! We're all crazy! There's crazyskip and crazymike! I'm crazywags."

"I'm going to be crazytrey," my roommate supplies, having come up for air. "How cool is that?"

The sad part is I don't want to do this. I don't want to be a brother. I don't want to be crazyvince. And now I have to, because I'd never be able to explain to Tommy that these poor guys didn't reject me. And then God only knows what he might do to them! Probably nothing, but how can I take the chance?

"Okay," I say with a sad shrug. "When it's time for spring rush, just tell me what I have to do."

I stand there for a long time, accepting his thanks, and willing him not to cry.

With effort, Trey pries himself away from Willow and exits the car. "Hang on, Vince. I'll walk with you."

Waghorn takes his place in the front seat, and he and Willow drive off.

"Still hot and heavy with you two," I observe.

But Trey's perma-grin has mysteriously faded. "I found out why the old man sent me that suit," he growls as we head for the dorm. "He does this all the time. He's got a big media event coming up, and I have to be there so he can play family man."

I shrug. "He's a politician. Image is everything in that business. What's wrong with helping him out a little?"

"It's so sleazy," Trey complains. "The Southern California Concrete Workers Union is having an election next month, and it's already getting nasty. The guy who's president now—he just disappeared, him and his driver. They could be kidnapped, or murdered. It's a tragedy! But here's Congressman Sutter, the great public servant, and all he sees is a way to get his name in the paper."

I'm confused. "What's a congressman got to do with some union kerfuffle?"

"He's put himself in it. He's going to mediate the dispute and oversee the election. Maybe he thinks he can ride in on a white horse and rescue the kidnapped guys."

"It sounds like he's trying to do a good thing," I reason.

Trey's voice is thick with sarcasm. "Oh, yeah. Picture thirty thousand concrete workers, all beating each other with clubs, while my dad's holding a press conference. And there I am in a Hugo Boss suit. I don't think so."

I hold my tongue. There's no talking to Trey where his father is concerned. But I do have one thought: How good a mediator can Representative Sutter be? He certainly can't make peace between himself and his own son.

We take the elevator to the fourth floor, and start up the bell-tower steps. At room 601, Trey fishes around for his key.

I grab his arm. "Did you forget to lock up?"

Our door stands slightly ajar.

Trey shakes his head. "What about Tommy?"

"Tommy drove down to Mexico. He won't be back until late," I whisper.

Gingerly, I push the door open, and we venture inside. The sight that awaits us is the kind that takes years off your life expectancy. There's an intruder in there, all right. We can see him through the wide-open door of our bathroom. He's sitting on the toilet, his pants draped around his feet, a large racing form concealing his identity.

Trey is tongue-tied, but not me. "What the hell is going on here?"

The paper flips down. He's smoking a cigar, too. "Great to see you, kid. How's college?"

It's one of my "uncles." In fact, this guy goes by the name Uncle Uncle.

The *what are you doing?* dies on my lips. I

don't want to hear about what he's doing. My question is, why is he doing it *here*?

A foot comes out of the pile of pants at the base of the john and kicks the door shut. "I'll be with you in a minute, Vince."

Trey drags me across the room. "Who's that?"

"My Uncle Uncle," I reply. "Don't ask. Everybody calls him that. He's—visiting."

That's when I notice the hot plate. A big pot of penne is boiling there. The microwave beeps, and I open it to find a steaming tub of *puttanesca* sauce.

"My mother's," I explain. "She won't let anyone come west without bringing a care package."

The toilet flushes, and Uncle Uncle emerges, looking dubiously around the room. "So this is Hollywood, huh?"

Now that his pants are on, I have the guts to ask him the purpose of this surprise visit.

"I'm a tourist," he replies. "Can you believe I've never seen California?"

I'd believe he's never seen New Jersey. The guy's entire life exists between his apartment in Howard Beach, JFK airport, where he and his crew help themselves to a lot of stuff, and the Rockville Centre home of Uncle Carmine. That's where a percentage of the take begins its journey up the ladder to Anthony Luca.

Uncle Uncle lives in a four-hundred-square-foot apartment, and drives the same car he received as a gift on his sixteenth birthday. He owns no TV; he has no phone. He wants nothing, needs nothing, and knows even less.

This guy has traveled three thousand miles to be a tourist? I sincerely doubt it.

Why has Anthony Luca sent one of his most trusted captains out to California?

CHAPTER SEVEN

IN A FAIR AND just society, P. Richard Shapiro would be skinned alive with a potato peeler and dipped in a vat of sulfuric acid.

Okay, that's a little extreme. But how come he gets to hang out with Kendra, and I don't?

It's been *weeks*, and I still haven't spent so much as five minutes alone with my own girl-friend. When Beth isn't around, P-Rick is. Or some other *Burnt Offering* cast member.

Can you believe it? While I can't seem to get any kind of project off the ground, P-Rick's dumb musical is not only up and humming, but the rehearsal and shooting schedule has ground my love life to a total halt.

I catch a glimpse of the script in Kendra's dorm

room. The thing is sixty-seven pages long! There are song lyrics, and dance numbers, and reams of dialogue detailing the merry mix-ups of Abraham, Sarah, and their biblical band of nomadic pranksters.

```
                  ABRAHAM
               (eyes heavenward)
     Haven't I always obeyed you, Lord?
     Circumcision--you think I was
     thrilled about it? Isaac and Ishmael
     sure didn't look too happy when I
     came at them with that rock. . . .
```

"Vince!" Kendra is horrified. "Put down that script!"

"I'm in the guy's class," I explain. "I'll be seeing the whole thing soon enough."

"Richard wants to keep everything under wraps until the premiere."

Did you catch that? The rest of us can stick a tape in a machine and hit PLAY, but that's not good enough for P-Rick. He has to have a premiere.

There is one benefit to Kendra having no time for me. At least she and Tommy won't be locking horns. I'm not worried about him being rude to her. In fact, he treats her with a lot of respect, mostly because he's scared to death of her. When

Tommy sees Kendra, it's like he's standing before the entire assembled staff of the FBI.

They do meet a few times—at least they brush past each other on the claustrophobic stairs of the bell tower. She's usually coming from a cast meeting in 801. I'm just grateful that she pokes her head in my door to say hello before heading home to Pacific Palisades.

"Hi, Tommy," she greets him.

"What's up?" he mumbles back, and the moment usually ends there. I'm starting to believe that Tommy really is going straight. Back in New York, a ten-second face-to-face with Kendra used to bring on hours of agonizing over what she might report to her father.

Speaking of society's newest law-abiding member, my brother seems genuinely amazed to find that Uncle Uncle is in town, staying at a posh hotel that costs more per night than his monthly rent in Howard Beach.

"Are you kidding? That guy's barely ever made it out of Queens!"

Tommy had such a great time in Mexico that he stayed three days. The only reason he came back when he did is—get this—he has a *date*! Just like a regular human. My brother is taking Zora out to dinner. I guess if you find a girl who isn't scared off by a gun in your belt, she's a keeper.

Because she's one of my foreign students, I feel a responsibility to protect her. "She's a stranger in a strange country," I warn him. "If you do anything to hurt her, I'll kill you."

He laughs. "She's not afraid of me. Where she comes from, they got timberwolves running wild in the streets, eating people."

I stare at him. "In Slovakia?"

He shrugs. "I'll treat her good. I promise."

"Like you promised to stay away from the frat house?"

He refuses to admit any wrongdoing. "You got in, didn't you?"

"I don't want to be in!"

To his credit, Tommy is a perfect gentleman with Zora, because he's on our floor, asleep and snoring, when I get home from a special screening of *Battleship Potemkin* for Film History class that night.

That's better than I can say for Trey, who's spending huge chunks of time with Willow, and barely coming home at all. But instead of his usual level of ultrahappiness, he's getting moodier and more tightly wound as his father's press conference approaches.

I have to admit that everything my roommate predicted has come true with a vengeance. The

California newscasts may as well change their names to the Congressman Sutter Hour. He's on CNN more often than Wolf Blitzer, and his picture is plastered on every front page and magazine cover.

With union leader Ellis Rank and his driver, Toothpick Anderson, still missing, Trey's dad is considered the only hope of keeping the union together without bloodshed.

To be honest, I'm kind of impressed to have met William Sutter. He's really the newsmaker of the moment. And unlike the people in *my* father's world, he's famous for the *right* reasons.

The press conference is scheduled for Friday morning. Trey begs me not to go to witness his humiliation as "a stooge for the old man's publicity machine." I go anyway, for support, and because I'm genuinely interested. The Rank story is a real mystery. What happened to the union boss and his driver? Were they kidnapped? Murdered? Or did they just take off?

In order to attend, I have to skip the rescreening of *Battleship Potemkin*, but I can't bear to sleep through it again, so that's okay.

The press conference is at the Winkler Auditorium on La Cienega. I'm meeting Willow there at 9:30. Trey has told her to stay away too, but she has the same idea as me. He needs us.

I'm brushing my teeth that morning when the phone rings. It's Trey, and I can tell right away that something's off.

"Where are you? With your dad?"

"Not exactly. I'm at the fourteenth precinct."

I'm shocked. "The police station? Why?" But even as I say it, I already know why. "You swiped something? *Today?*"

I picture his back stiffening. "There's nothing special about today just because the old man is having a press conference."

But there is, and we both know it.

"I didn't mean it like that," I say quickly. "I just meant—it's eight o'clock in the morning! Where did you find a store that was even open?"

His tone is cold. "The Home Depot in Marina del Rey is open twenty-four hours."

"What can I do to help you, Trey? I don't know any lawyers or bail bondsmen. I don't know what to do to get you out."

His answer is weird. "Don't do anything. They told me I had one phone call, so I called you."

I'm horrified. "You mean you haven't even called your dad yet?"

I can almost hear the smile. "Someone'll tell him. Eventually."

"*I'll* tell him right now!" I promise. "What's his number?"

"The great William Sutter? You can't bother him. He's king of the world today. But do me a favor, Vince. Make sure Willow knows not to go to the press conference. I won't be there. And—oh, yeah—don't wait up." *Click.*

"Trey, wait—"

I don't even take time to think about it. I just throw on clothes, print MapQuest directions to the fourteenth precinct, and pound downstairs to my Mazda, choking on a stale breadstick by way of breakfast.

The route takes me within a couple of blocks of the Winkler Auditorium. You can see that the parking lot is already starting to fill up, and several mobile TV units are in place.

My head is spinning so fast it's a wonder I can see to drive. My father is a Mob boss. My brother brings a pistol to my freshman video shoot. My "uncle" commits breaking and entering so he can use the commode. And who am I going to try to bail out of jail? The blue-blood son of a United States congressman.

For a city of beautiful beaches, movie stars, glitz, and incredible wealth, L.A.'s police stations are pretty drab. The parking lot is so cramped that

I scratch the Mazda's bumper against a post on the way in. That must be my punishment for violating the number-one Luca family axiom: never go to a cop shop on purpose. (Dad's attitude is, if they want you, they'll come and get you—which they frequently do.)

"I'm looking for Trey Sutter," I tell the sergeant.

But then I see him at a desk. If I wasn't so upset, I'd laugh at the sight of him.

He's wearing that fifteen-hundred-dollar Hugo Boss suit, straight out of the box. And there isn't a square centimeter of the fabric that doesn't have at least one wrinkle. He looks like a homeless person who pulled some clothes out of Donald Trump's garbage.

He's slumped in his chair, more bored than intimidated. Beside him stands the evidence against him: a gourmet Weber deluxe propane barbecue grill cart.

I'm dumbfounded. "That's what you stole? *That*? Are you crazy?"

His cat-that-ate-the-canary grin tells me everything I need to know. This was no snatch and grab, just for the thrill of it. He did this on purpose to get caught.

I take a stab at it. "Is he free to go?"

There's a young officer sitting opposite Trey. "Let me check my criminal code. Stealing . . . stealing . . . yep, here it is. Still illegal." He glares at me. "No, he's not free to go."

Trey smiles uncomfortably. I'm sorry for him. Even though he has brought it on himself, it can't be fun to be under arrest. But what can I do to help? I'm not a lawyer, I have no bail money—

Then it hits me. I'm embarrassed to say it, but there have been times in my life where certain doors have been opened to me based on who my dad is. Well, Trey has the same thing, only better. He refuses to play that card, but that doesn't mean I can't play it for him.

"Listen, officer," I plead, "this is William Sutter's only son. You've got to find a way to get in touch with the congressman. He's scheduled to go on at the Winkler Auditorium in less than an hour. And Trey is supposed to be sitting right next to him."

Hey, you don't grow up in a house with the FBI listening in on every Scrabble game without knowing how to direct the attention of a bunch of cops. Their lieutenant gets on the horn with the congressman's LAPD security detail.

The limo is at the door of the fourteenth precinct in ten minutes.

Trey is not happy with me. "You shouldn't have

done that, Vince. This is none of your business."

But I know I've done the right thing.

Representative Sutter appears in the station house, with an entourage of about half a dozen. He approaches his son, and I hold my breath. What will he do? Yell at him? Hit him? Or break down and hug him?

None of the above. Instead, he gives him an ironic half smile. "A barbecue, huh? That would have come in handy in your sixth-floor dorm room."

Trey is tight-lipped. "I thought you had a press conference."

"*We* have a press conference."

It's interesting to watch the congressman operate. By the time he's done, he has all those cops believing that stealing barbecues is a rite of passage for all college freshmen. He signs autographs and poses for a few pictures. Apparently, Trey's dad is a big supporter of the state Fraternal Order of Police, well liked in law enforcement circles.

When it comes time for him and Trey to walk out the front door, no one seems to remember that the kid in the rumpled suit is supposedly being charged with a crime. Home Depot is getting its barbecue back, right? All the rest is just a pile of details.

Representative Sutter turns to me as they get into the limo. "Thanks a lot for the heads-up, Vince. We owe you."

It's only a few words, but I go warm all over. A member of the United States Congress appreciates what I've done for him and his son. The permanent background guilt over my entire life being funded by organized crime is suddenly lighter than air, and I feel totally, amazingly worthwhile.

I drive out of there without even brooding over the scratch on my Mazda.

CHAPTER EIGHT

THE WINKLER AUDITORIUM is packed. Every jobsite in Southern California must be shut down. If you work with concrete, you're here.

There are two factions. The red banners bear the name and likeness of Ellis Rank, who looks like a hulking Caucasian Yoda, with bulging eyes behind heavy-rimmed glasses. They're an angry-looking lot, these Rank supporters, probably because their candidate has disappeared. And they're suspicious of the guys with the green banners, supporters of Pat McCracken, the union leader who is hoping to replace Rank.

The atmosphere is really tense, and kind of scary. These are big tough people, and a lot of them are holding signs on suspiciously sturdy sticks. Although none of them has any quarrel with me, I'd hate to be caught in the crossfire if green and red decide to take out their frustration on each other.

But Congressman Sutter! The guy is amazing. Suddenly, all eyes are on him, and even the tone of his voice oozes reason and conciliation. He sounds confident and in control, but at the same time not autocratic or overbearing. He isn't telling the concrete workers how to run their union, but he's using his skill as a communicator and a mediator to help the members focus on their common goals and dreams rather than their differences.

His plan is to have one of Rank's top lieutenants, a man named Dooley, stand in for the missing president in the election. It's a hard sell, because it's asking the Rank supporters to write off the leader they believe in.

On a row of chairs behind the podium sit Dooley and McCracken, also Trey's mom, and beside her, the barbecue bandit himself. Somehow, in the last twenty minutes, the Hugo Boss suit has been pressed. This, more than the speech or anything else, convinces me that William Sutter is a miracle worker.

I'm pretty absorbed in this, watching the union guys watch Sutter. And all at once, I realize that I know someone in the big room, and not just on the stage, either. On the far side of the auditorium, at the apron of the floor, a sign gets raised a little higher, revealing a familiar face.

What's Uncle Uncle doing here?

My mind races. Okay, I never believed the guy was in L.A. on vacation, but this makes no sense at all. Just as I'm mulling that one over, I spot Uncle No-Nose a few rows in front of me. No-Nose is a collector for my father's loan-sharking operation. What's he doing at a California union meeting?

It's almost like once you find Waldo the first time, he's everywhere. Uncle Fingers is by the central pillar. Gus the Greek, from his crew, stands like a sentinel at the north exit. I turn to the south exit. Rafael, one of Uncle Uncle's guys. All Luca people, all here.

Just as I'm turning this disturbing development over in my head, something smells good, and warm breath blows in my ear. "Hey, sexy."

Oh, boy. I forgot all about Willow. But it's understandable, right? This has been a hectic morning.

"I'm sorry I didn't call. I—uh—overslept."

If she's angry, she hides it well. She looks me right in the eyes and, with a sultry smile, says, "I hope it was a good dream."

Okay, an auditorium full of agitated construction workers isn't the most romantic place in the world. But this is Willow. She could raise your heart rate in a hovercraft full of eels. She almost makes me forget that this place is salted with my father's goons.

So not only do I have to grapple with that strange fact, but I have to do it with her pulling my chain.

"It's been an odd morning," I inform her. "Trey'll probably tell you about it later."

She lightly brushes her fingers where my biceps would be if I had biceps. "Been working out?"

Terrific. She's determined to put me through this, here of all places, now of all times.

"You know," I sigh, "it's okay that you and Trey are together. I can handle it."

"You have really nice eyes."

Has she no mercy? "Willow—"

She grabs my arm. "This is boring. Let's get out of here."

"We're here to support Trey," I remind her.

"*I'm* here to see you."

Her lips are on mine so fast it's like a jump cut. Right there, with her boyfriend not half a football field away, she kisses me so thoroughly that, at this moment, I couldn't pick Kendra out of a lineup. The contact is softer, smoother; it tastes different, smells different. More—womanly.

Who knows how far it might have gone if it wasn't for the riot?

I have no idea how it starts. Let's face it—at this moment, I wouldn't notice an atomic blast. But when Willow pulls back from me, there's a free-for-all going on. Angry shouts are swelling to a roar, fists and chairs are flying, and all those red and green signs have reverted to the purpose for which they were probably intended: weapons. It looks like the battle scene from *A Cro-Magnon Christmas*.

Congressman Sutter tries valiantly to restore order, but the security people insist on escorting the dais party out. I catch a glimpse of Trey just before he disappears through the stage door. The expression on his face is pure bliss. His father's press conference has degenerated into a brawl, and he didn't even have to get arrested to make it happen.

"I've had a crush on you from the moment I met you!" Willow calls, struggling to hold her position amid the surging masses. Her raising her voice to be heard lends her message a special absurdity, like a sketch on *Saturday Night Live*. "When I'm with Trey, I'm thinking about you!"

I'm struck dumb. All the flirting, the suggestive remarks, compliments on muscles I don't have. It never even crossed my mind she might be *serious*.

"But—"

A very large airborne concrete worker sails by where my head was a split second before. It's a scary situation, but it must be even scarier for poor Willow, who's a lot smaller than I am. I grab her and join the crowd pushing toward the nearest exit.

"I have a girlfriend!" I yell as we bob and stumble.

A flailing elbow belts me full in the face, and by the time I recover, the roiling crowd has carried me twenty feet off course. "Willow!"

She's gone, and I'm carried along by an inexorable tide, my vision blocked by big shoulders in every direction. The soundtrack is the sickening thud of fist meeting nose, cranium meeting plywood. The cursing is a vocabulary lesson. If you think these guys are tough, you should hear what their mothers have allegedly been up to.

It's probably only seven or eight minutes, but it seems like a lifetime before I'm squeezed out through the emergency exit. I breathe the fresh air only for a second. The cops have a fleet of paddy wagons waiting, and I'm shoved into the first of them. Just before the doors slam shut in my face, I catch a glimpse of Willow out on the street. The policeman who is releasing her is grinning like an idiot. I know exactly where that guy is coming from.

And there, standing on the bus, packed in between bruised and bleeding concrete workers, I remember a chapter on the history of organized labor from a high school civics book. In the fifties and sixties, it was common practice for organized crime to manipulate the unions. The number-one tactic was to send in a few rabble-rousers to stir up tension in mass meetings until violence broke out.

I've got to say it rings a bell. I didn't see how this riot started, but I'm willing to bet money that the first punches were thrown by Uncle Uncle, Uncle No-Nose, Uncle Fingers, Rafael, and Gus the Greek.

I look around, but I don't see any of the Luca people on this paddy wagon, or in the groups being herded onto the others. That was also in the civics books. The Mob instigators would start the fists flying, and then melt away and let the poor slobs fight.

I feel a nervous tightening in the pit of my stomach, one that has nothing to do with the fact that I'm under arrest. The mystery of what my father's people are suddenly doing "on vacation" in

L.A. is no longer a mystery. And what about Tommy? His sudden interest in getting out of The Life is pretty conveniently timed to act as a smoke-screen for his involvement in this nasty affair. The Luca organization is somehow mixed up in California union politics. Which means I have come three thousand miles to get away from my father's business only to have my father's business follow me.

That's bad enough, but there's a darker, even more serious side to all this. If Anthony Luca is mixed up in the concrete-workers' election, is he also involved in the disappearance of Ellis Rank and his driver, Toothpick Anderson?

As it turns out, nobody is arrested. The cops just want to cool everybody off for a while before releasing us. As luck would have it, I end up at the fourteenth precinct again.

"Hey, aren't you the guy who came in with Sutter's kid?" asks the desk sergeant. "You're a busy boy today."

They make fun of me, but at least I'm out of there fast, before anyone looks at my New York driver's license and wonders if I'm related to the vending machine king of the East Coast.

I spend just enough time in custody to gain an

understanding of what Trey's dad is up against. The Ellis Rank supporters don't see why they should have to vote for Dooley just because their real candidate may be a victim of foul play. Pat McCracken's people ask, What if they elect a president who turns out to be dead? Or hiding in South America? It's more than an honest difference of opinion. The two sides are accusing each other of fraud, kidnapping—even murder!

Getting those two factions together would be hard enough under the best of circumstances. With Anthony Luca's thugs deliberately stirring up trouble, it's going to be next to impossible. If Congressman Sutter can work all this out, I figure him for the Nobel Peace Prize, not to mention a red *S* on his chest.

I have to walk back to the auditorium to get my car, so it's late afternoon by the time I get to the dorm. I feel as if this day has already lasted millennia as I open the door.

"What the—"

There, draped in various poses around our sparse furniture, sit Uncles No-Nose, Fingers, and Uncle, along with Rafael, Gus the Greek, and a guy they call the Pope. I must have missed him at the press conference. In the middle of the floor, handing out cold beers from an ice-filled wastebasket, is Tommy, their gracious host.

A great welcoming cheer of *"Vince!"* goes up in the room. Everybody's smiling and laughing, good humor abounds—it's a full-fledged celebration.

The only cloud on the horizon is me. "I'm on to you guys! I saw what you did at that union thing!"

Uncle No-Nose gives me the wide-eyed innocence. "Couldn't have been us, kid. We were at Knott's Berry Farm."

Oh, right. Six New York mobsters, the quintessential tourists at Knott's Berry Farm. Tomorrow: Disneyland.

"Must've been a bunch of guys who look like them," adds Tommy.

I turn on my brother. "And you! Were you there too? You were part of this operation from the beginning, right? That was just a cover story, all that stuff about taking a whiz on Shlomo's Hummer!"

The Pope is impressed. "You took a whiz on Shlomo's Hummer? Man, he loves that car!"

Uncle Uncle frowns. "You mean Shlomo from Ozone Park, or Shlomo from Kings Highway?"

"Kings Highway Shlomo drives a Range Rover," puts in Uncle Fingers.

"I think there's a couple more Shlomos out in Jersey somewhere," offers Gus.

I know what's happening. These guys aren't as dumb as they look. No, strike that. They're *exactly* as dumb as they look, but they can also be kind of sharp in a streetwise way. They're keeping me in the dark. They wouldn't tell me anything if I put flaming bamboo under their fingernails.

A key jingles in the lock, and Trey walks in on this theater of the absurd. He's still wearing the Hugo Boss and the grin he got from watching his father's press conference combust, thanks to present company.

He looks delighted to see everybody. "Whoa—party!"

"No, it isn't," I say pointedly. I make a few sketchy introductions and add, "They're on vacation." Another amazing thing about Dad's business: I always end up using the very same lies that are used on me.

Trey helps himself to a beer. "You caught me at a good time. Something big went really well for me today."

"Us, too." Uncle Fingers beams.

Eight hundred beers and four pizzas later, not one of those guys has left yet. Trey won't let them. He's in his glory, shmoozing, promising to show them L.A., and lecturing about "making the city work for you."

Uncle Uncle sighs. "You kids have the life. I never made it to college."

Who does he think he's kidding? He never made it to middle school!

And before my eyes, all those mobsters are lamenting the outrageous fortune that robbed them of the university experience. Including Tommy, who, I know for a fact, couldn't wait for his sixteenth birthday so he could drop out of eleventh grade.

"I don't miss the learning part so much," he says wistfully. "There's more to education than books. But I feel like I got rooked out of the lifestyle: the good times, the laughs, the chicks, the hell-raising . . ."

Trey's bleary eyes light up. "I can help you with that! What do you say we raise some hell right now?"

"I've got a test tomorrow," I announce loudly.

"Come on, Vince," my brother protests. "It's just getting interesting." He turns to Trey. "What've you got in mind, kid?"

Trey thinks it over. "Let's get, like, twenty rolls of toilet paper. We'll go over to the dean's house and wrap it up like a Christmas present!"

The uncles stare at him blankly.

"And—?" prompts Gus.

"Don't you get it?" Trey crows. "Tomorrow morning, Dr. Kazak wakes up, and he can't get out the front door!"

Uncle Uncle breaks the uncomfortable silence. "How about this. We go to the house, knock on the door, and say, 'Listen, you got a nice house here. It'd be a shame to see it wrapped in toilet paper. But for just a few bucks, we'll keep an eye on the place to make sure it never happens.'"

Now it's Trey's turn to look blank. "Where's the fun in that?"

Uncle No-Nose puts an arm around his shoulders. "What's your major, kid?"

"Business," Trey replies.

I stand up. "I'm calling Dad."

The room is cleared in thirty seconds.

CHAPTER NINE

"LET ME GET THIS straight," Alex says over the phone. "You made out with your roommate's girlfriend?"

It's Monday morning, and Trey has gone to an early class. I'm alone, but I still feel funny talking about this out loud, as if the walls have ears. Maybe it comes from growing up in a bugged house.

"It happened so fast I couldn't stop it," I tell him. "Trust me, I feel awful about it."

Alex sees it a different way. "Dammit, Vince, you have all the luck! Kendra puts you on ice, and before your teeth start chattering, an even hotter chick is firing up the burner!"

I don't even know where to begin. "First of all, Kendra didn't put me on ice. She's just busy, that's all. And this thing with Willow—it's never going to happen again. You know, as a best friend, you stink! I have no idea why I tell you stuff!"

"What did Kendra say about the kiss?" he prods.

"She said nothing, and for a very good reason. I didn't tell her, and she's never going to find out any other way, right?"

"Not smart," Alex clucks. "Willow is *leverage*. It's like saying to Kendra, 'Play me or trade me.' There are other teams in this league that won't have you riding the bench."

"Oh, stop it," I groan. "What's happening on your end? How was it bunking with Frankie?"

"You mean how *is* it," he corrects me. "He's still here."

I'm amazed. "How long does it take to paint an apartment?"

"Turns out it's a whole renovation," Alex explains. "Knocking down a wall, changing some plumbing—you know how these contractors can be."

"Do you have space for the guy?" I ask. "How big is your dorm room?"

"Small, but there's a gigantic walk-in closet. He sleeps on a mattress in there." He hesitates. "The only bad part is the poor guy is so depressed about being homeless that he's not doing much business. Remember the hot-chick river? Well, it's more like a dry wash. We hardly even go out anymore."

I go out, I think to myself. I go to riots. I go to jail. Maybe I should take a page from Frankie's book and stay home.

Because the call drags on, I'm late for my work-study job. I burst through the film-school doors, hoping against hope that I won't see a throng of foreign students lined up outside my cubicle, the usual mixture of anxiety and cluelessness on their faces.

Sure enough, the usual suspects are crowded around my desk. But they look fascinated, engaged, admiring. Tommy sits in my chair, his sleeves rolled up, delving through stacks of open books.

He glances disapprovingly up at me. "Hey, Vince, you're not really doing your job here."

"Oh, yeah?" I reply coldly. Funny my brother should know so much about it, considering that he's never held a job in his life.

"L.A. is a pricey town, especially when your life savings is in shekels and junk like that," Tommy explains. "But there are all these grants out there."

I'm skeptical. "What kind of grants?"

"Grants. From their home countries. Not

SOUTH BURLINGTON COMM. LIBRARY
540 Dorset Street
South Burlington, VT 05403

millions—just a few bucks here and there to make sure they're not eating dog food while getting educated." He hands me a page. "Like this one. The Dalai Lama International Scholarship Fund. Three grand. I don't know why they named a scholarship after a dumb animal, but, hey—three large is three large."

I skim the guidelines. "That's 'for a student *of Tibetan origin,*' Tommy! You have to be from Tibet."

He shrugs it off and tosses that page into the wastebasket. "Lots of other places here—Costa Rica . . . Madagascar . . . Uzbekistan . . . Mozambique . . ."

"Cobi is from there," puts in Zora.

Tommy is triumphant. "You see? Twenty-five hundred bucks for sitting on his can."

I'm surprised and a little ashamed. When Tommy has an idea, my knee-jerk reaction is to assume it's a scam. But he's right. A lot of my foreign students have trouble making ends meet. Most of their visas won't allow them to work, and savings don't go very far in an expensive town like Santa Monica.

"I think you might be on to something," I concede.

Tommy's offended. "I may not be Joe College

like you, but I know a thing or two about getting money. And when people are so desperate to give it away that they put ads in magazines, you've got to have your head examined if you're not the first guy in line."

Who can argue with that? "Okay," I say. "Everybody—write down your home countries, and I'll check to see if there's anything available for you."

There's so much hemming, hawing, and throat clearing that I look up from the book. "What?"

Rahim breaks the silence. "Well, Vince, this is a pretty important thing. We prefer to let Tommy handle it."

"We like you," Zora adds quickly, "but you are here for answering phones. Your brother, he has the real business experience."

Yeah, loan-sharking, hijacking trucks, breaking heads. If they're planning to threaten the grant administrator with kneecapping, my brother is the man.

On the other hand, why am I being so sensitive? Tommy's only trying to help, probably because he likes Zora and wants to impress her. Considering the string of bimbos he's dated in the past, I should be happy to see him interested in a normal nice girl. And if he can wangle my foreign students some extra cash in the process, so much the better.

Besides, even if nothing ever comes of it, this search for college grants is a lot like a real job. If Tommy's serious about going straight, at some point he'll have to figure out what he wants to do with his life. This could be the first step.

"Can I sit at my desk at least?" I request. "You know, just in case Carl checks to see if I'm working?"

Tommy lifts his broad beam out of my chair. "It's all yours, Vince. I'm taking the gang to the library. They've got to have tons of grant books there." And my brother marches out of the office, acolytes in tow: the Pied Piper with a snub-nosed revolver instead of a flute. I wonder if they've noticed yet that he still hasn't taken it back to the props department.

So I've got my desk back—my whole cubicle, in fact. But the irony is that, with no foreign students around, I've got nothing to do. The phone doesn't ring. Why would it? My best customers are all on their way to the library. And pretty soon my brother will be calling the rest of the department, spreading the good news that there's a fortune waiting for them in the coffers of the Joe Blow Educational Foundation for the Terminally Ugly.

Easy, Vince, I tell myself. Tommy's doing something positive, and that's a welcome change. Besides, I should be happy to have a moment to think, without Trey, or Willow, or Alex, or the uncles driving me crazy in new and exciting ways.

Did you ever find yourself looking at something, and when you finally notice what you're doing, you've been staring at it for a long time? It's at least twenty minutes before it hits me that my gaze has been focused straight out the window on the pay phone at the corner.

I suddenly know what's been on my mind for days. I call home on a regular basis, mostly to talk to Mom and assure her that I've been eating regularly. I talk to Dad too—about the weather, the sports news, and how my classes are coming along. But if I have something to say—and I have *many* things to say to him right now—I can't, because the line could be bugged by the FBI. That includes my dorm phone, my cell phone, and possibly even my work phone. There's only one way to have a real conversation with my father: pay phone to pay phone.

I mumble something to Carl about a family emergency, and race out to the street. I stick in all the change I have and dial Dad's private cell.

When he answers, I say, "Write this down—" and give him the pay phone number.

He says, "Ten minutes."

I wait, hoping that Carl won't glance out the window and see me having my family emergency all alone in a phone booth.

It's ten minutes to the second when my father calls. There are traffic noises in the background, and—is that thunder?

"This'd better be good."

I fire the opening salvo. "A few friends of yours are in town, Dad."

"I think it's great," he says evenly. "Those guys work too hard. I've been worried Uncle was going to live and die in that crackerbox in Howard Beach. A change of scenery will do them all some good."

"Yeah, well, maybe they're not relaxing as much as you think," I drawl. "When I first saw them, they were at a union meeting, which isn't listed in many of the tourist books. And by the time it was over . . ." Talking to Dad can be exhausting. It's like a chess match, and I can't think that many moves ahead. So I just say it outright: "Well, I guess you already know how it ended. You ordered it to happen."

"Here's a question," my father says coldly. "What were *you* doing at a union meeting? Thirty-five grand a year, you should be studying. You should be watching *Battleship Potemkin*."

That stops me in my tracks. How could Dad know I cut the rescreening to go to the press conference? He must have Tommy giving him updates from the film school syllabus!

I go on the offensive. "What happened to Ellis Rank and Toothpick Anderson?"

He's getting irritated. "You tell me, Vince, because according to CNN, nobody knows."

"I'll bet *you* know." If he knows about *Battleship Potemkin*, he knows everything.

I hear him sigh. "Do we have to do this again? You don't want any part of my business. Fine. But if you want to be out of it, stay out of it!"

"So you admit that Ellis Rank is part of your business!"

"I admit that it's raining cats and dogs here, and I'm out of quarters!" he barks. "So just this once, I'm going to break my rule and let you ask a question you have no right to ask, and I shouldn't have to answer. Fire away."

I take a deep breath. "Did you make Ellis Rank disappear?"

He's ready with the answer. "No, I didn't. Happy?"

"And that's the truth?" I persist.

An automated voice butts in. *"Please insert sixty-five cents."* I don't hear any more coins drop.

"The next time I talk to you," my father warns, "it had better be about *Battleship Potemkin*."

And with a click, he's gone.

I go back to the office and slump down at my desk, feeling even more unsettled. Whatever gave me the idea that talking to Dad would put my mind at rest?

Is he leveling with me? As mobsters go, my father is considered the straightest arrow in the quiver. Honest Abe Luca, they call him.

Do I believe him? I'd like to. Then I see the uncles sprinkled throughout the Winkler Auditorium, and I know they aren't there for the refined company and quality entertainment.

If they're in it, so is Dad, which means he's lying. But then why did he go out of his way to invite me to ask him the question like that? Anthony Luca is a master subject changer, an accomplished obfuscator, a magnificent conjurer of smoke screens. Yet he practically begged me for the opportunity to say he didn't do it. It doesn't make sense.

Maybe the real problem is me. One of the things that has always landed me in trouble over the years is I think like a civilian in the organized crime world. It's more than possible that there's no such thing as the pure truth in a business where friendship, loyalty, and fairness mean nothing, might makes right, and the only issue that matters is, *What's in it for me?* Maybe in Dad's mind, he can lie and tell the truth at the same time, just the way light can simultaneously be both a wave and a particle.

I don't know what to think.

CHAPTER TEN

I'M STANDING IN the bathroom of room 701, my head obscured by a thick fog of salon products.

"Your hair's thin where it should be full," Alitalia complains. "But where it needs to lie down, it stands up."

Luca locks—designed for a fistful of grease, not anything the Revlon corporation has to offer.

Anorexia snips at me with a small scissors. "Let me trim the poofy parts and flatten the sides with gel."

"Don't do it, Vince!" Perry's voice warns through the heating duct. "They'll shave you down to a brainstem!" The vents up here work better than a fiber-optic communications network.

"What would you know about having a brain?" Alitalia fires back mildly.

I hear grumbling from below. It's been a tough day in 501. Earlier, Calvin had a false Ringo sighting that turned out to be just some guy watering the plants. His disappointment was enough to wilt the bell tower.

But nothing could spoil this night for me. After a month in California, I have a date with Kendra. It'll be our first real time alone together since the start of college.

I thank the girls and run down to my room, which I have to myself tonight. Trey's back home in Orange County, which signifies that he's run out of underwear and needs to do laundry. To say I'm pumped is an understatement. I set aside how pathetic it is that I have to jump through hoops to take out my own girlfriend, and head for Pacific Palisades.

Seeing her is pure magic. All the pressures of college, and dorm life, and P-Rick's video evaporate. It's the old days again, when not even our families could come between us.

As much as I'm tempted to spend the entire duration of the date in the backseat of my car, we grab dinner in West Hollywood, and wend our way up Sunset, finally settling in a small, dark jazz club called Riffs.

The place turns out to be great, with a blues

combo alternating with a Norah Jones wannabe on piano. Kendra's eating it up, nuzzling closer with every number. "This is perfect, Vince," she mumbles in my ear. "You know me so well."

"Yeah." It's a triple bull's-eye: hip, urban, and musical—everything she came west for. I transmit my psychic thanks to Trey, who recommended the joint.

We're cocooned in a private corner, and I can tell the whole thing is about to degenerate into a prolonged make-out session—the best kind of entropy. Suits me just fine.

My mouth is on its way to hers, millimeters from the target, when a familiar voice declares, "Hey, sexy. It *is* you!"

It's another feature of Trey Sutter's L.A.— Willow.

She's about sixty percent crammed into a slinky knit minidress. I can't help gawking. It isn't even purely sexual. Part of me is just astounded at the feat of engineering that keeps such a small amount of fabric attached to her body.

"This is Willow, Trey's girlfriend. Willow—Kendra."

"Good to meet you." She pulls up a chair, completely at home. "I was afraid I wouldn't know anybody here. Is this place awesome or what?"

Well, how can I tell her to get lost? She orders a drink. The waiter is already flirting with her, but she doesn't even notice that he's staring at her legs instead of his notepad.

"Do you guys shoot pool? I was at this great place up the block. Lots of actors go there. Nobody super famous tonight—just this one soap-opera guy. You know *All My Children* . . . ?"

Sue me, I'm interested. This whole Hollywood thing is new to me. Kendra kicks me under the table.

I flash her a look. *She's a friend. She showed up. What can I do?*

My plan is to hang with Willow for one set, and then split with Kendra. But I get sucked in. I could chew the fat with Willow forever and never be bored. Seriously, there isn't a single subject the girl doesn't have interesting opinions about—sports, movies, philosophy, you name it. She's sexy, sure. But she's also the kind of person you stay up all night with, just yakking.

And it probably doesn't help that every guy in the place, from the age of eighteen to eighty, is checking Willow out. Soon free drinks start arriving, gifts from her many admirers. It isn't too long before we're facing the first suitor.

He's a real L.A. type. Dressed entirely in black,

thick dark hair—he looks like Zorro. Trey would probably say he's making the city work for him. In reality, he's an obnoxious loudmouth who's getting on Willow's nerves, and mine too.

You can tell she has a lot of experience brushing off losers. "You're sweet," she says to the guy, "but I'm here with people."

Kendra squeezes my arm. "This isn't fun. Let's go."

I'm stuck. How can I abandon Willow with Zorro hanging off her?

"I can't leave my friends," she replies to a question I don't quite catch. "Sorry."

The guy gets aggressive. He puts an arm around her shoulder, which Willow deftly deflects. But I've had enough. I grab Zorro by the collar and yank him to his feet. He's not happy—in fact, I think he's deciding whether or not to take a swing at me. I freeze him with the Luca Stare. Through an accident of heredity, I've acquired my father's fiercest look, the one that conveys all the violence Anthony Luca is capable of unleashing at a moment's notice. I've got none of the firepower in reality, but Zorro doesn't know that. He gives me the finger and slinks off into the cigarette smoke.

Deep breath. "Okay." For the moment, I'm the

Alpha male, and I take advantage of that temporary status. "Let's get out of here."

The Spanish Inquisition starts as soon as we deposit Willow in her car.

"You like her, don't you?"

"I don't have a lot of choice in the matter." I start up the Mazda. "She's Trey's girlfriend. I'm stuck with her. But, yeah, I do like her. She's a fun person."

"More fun than me?"

I pull out into traffic. "Not even in your league," I assure her, patting her knee.

She pushes my hand away. "She's beautiful."

This is the moment of truth. "Really?" I say nonchalantly. "Yeah, I suppose a lot of guys would find her attractive. If they're into that type."

She doesn't buy it. "You're jealous of Trey."

"The only reason I'm jealous of Trey is he gets to *see* his girlfriend. You're always too busy."

"You were ready to fight that guy. Would you do that for me?"

"Of course."

"You never have before."

"Because nobody ever hits on you."

Wrong answer. "I mean, they *would*," I babble, "but we don't hang out in places like that—you know, where dirtbags cruise for women. But if

Willow wasn't there, and the guy was hitting on you—not that dirtbags like *her* better, but *this* dirtbag—his personal taste—"

"Take me home, Vince."

Damage control. "That came out wrong—"

"Now."

I make a U-turn, reflecting that no situation is ever so bad that it can't get a whole lot worse.

The blender appears in our room as if by magic— the same magic by which it disappeared from the store, I'm sure.

When it starts to sink in that Congressman Sutter's political career isn't crashing because of the riot at the press conference, Trey's mood resumes its downward spiral. And the only way to help himself is to help himself. Which he does, to pretty much everything that isn't nailed down. Our room is starting to look like Macy's.

"You've got to take it easy, or you're going to get arrested again," I plead.

Talk to the wall. "Most politicians can't pass gas without being indicted for something. But nothing sticks to my old man. A giant riot, thanks to his lust for publicity, and the whole thing gets blamed on 'outside agitators.' You were there, Vince. Did you see any outside agitators?"

That depends on what he means by outside. Outside of the guest list from my first communion? No.

Speaking of the uncles, they've been stopping by quite a lot, to watch TV and hang around with us. That's why Trey needs the blender, to experiment with frozen drinks for them.

He doesn't seem to notice that they're not doing much tourism, or even that they're a little rough around the edges. Yesterday, he explained how they could go skiing in the morning and surfing in the afternoon. Instead, they slept past lunch and spent the rest of the day in our room, watching horse racing and calling in bets on their cell phones.

Betting—now there's a subject we have in common. I take out my Probability notes and hit them up for pointers on blackjack. They look at me as if I've just asked them to read the entrails of a goat.

"It's all math," I explain, pointing at Mr. Lai's columns of calculations. "See? This is the formula for the likelihood of pulling a face card."

"It's a game of chance, Vince," Tommy tells me. "Unless you stack the deck, you can't know what card is going to come up."

"Right," I agree. "But in blackjack, there are more tens than regular numbers. By understanding the probabilities, you can know when to bet high."

"I like the queen of diamonds," offers Gus. "She's sexier than the other queens. When I see the queen of diamonds, that's when I bet the farm."

"You're crazy," snorts Uncle No-Nose. "The queen of diamonds is a mutt. The queen of spades—now there's a woman."

"That's because you like brunettes," puts in Rafael.

I stash away my notes. Now I understand why wiseguys, who make tons of money, are perpetually broke.

Trey mixes piña coladas and plays host through all this, but his smile is looking more and more forced.

I feel guilty. "I'll tell them to find another hangout," I promise, figuring he's as sick of the uncles as I am. "I know it's not fair to you. This room is half yours, and they're all mine."

He looks surprised. "That's not it. I love those guys. It's Willow."

Uh-oh. "What's the problem with Willow?"

He shrugs miserably. "I don't know. Maybe nothing. This could be just a bad week. But lately I've been getting this vibe that she's not so into me anymore."

Come to think of it, I've noticed he hasn't been slinking home with those half-moon bite marks lately.

I genuinely sympathize. "I know what that's like, man. Ever since school started, I can't seem to get on the same page with Kendra."

"To be honest, *hombre*," he says earnestly, "I'm starting to get the feeling Willow's messing around with some other guy."

That's when the alarm bell goes off in my head. Please God, don't let it be me!

I'm innocent, of course. Except for that kiss at the press conference, my behavior has been saintly. But what about that night at the jazz place? In a city the size of L.A., it's a pretty big coincidence to just run into her. Could she have wheedled my destination out of Trey? And now she's frosting him because she's falling for me?

Oh, come on! I'm not putting myself down, but Willow is *Willow*! She's twenty-one years old, with the kind of looks that stand out even in a place like Hollywood, which is full of models and actresses. She could have anyone she wants. Why would she pick an eighteen-year-old freshman with no shoulders and pasty, pale skin from growing up in New York smog?

"This is just between you and me," Trey adds

confidentially. "You know, roommate to roommate."

The very next day, he spills his guts to Tommy.

"What happened to 'roommate to roommate'?" I ask him.

"He's a roommate's brother," Trey reasons. "What could be closer than that?"

Well, obviously six total strangers. When the uncles straggle in that night, we discuss the Willow situation in open forum.

It makes me uneasy. Even though I'm an outsider, I know how relationship issues are resolved in their world. But the mobsters don't seem interested in offering conflict resolution suggestions to Trey. They smile sympathetically, they nod. Uncle Fingers even clucks. But they keep their opinions to themselves.

Trey, though, won't let it die. "Come on, guys. You're all men of the world. Help me out, here."

And finally, Tommy obliges him with a few words of sage counsel: "Listen, Trey, a woman's brain is like the inside of a computer. Something's going on in there, but damned if you can ever figure out what. While it's working, it's just fine. And when it breaks down, don't even try to fix it. You'll just make yourself crazy. It's time for a new computer."

He gets a standing ovation from the uncles, but Trey still looks careworn.

"I don't think I can cut her loose like that. You don't know Willow. She's too awesome. I've got to find a way to make it work."

"In that case," Tommy concludes, "if you're positive she's two-timing you, there's only one thing to do. Find the guy."

I marvel. Mom says you can always count on family. Dad says it too, but he means something completely different. And me? I can count on my brother to come three thousand miles to set my roommate off on a blood feud—with me as the hunted.

So there's tension, no doubt about that. But believe it or not, it isn't the biggest source of stress in my life. The first projects for TV production class are due on Friday, and I haven't got an inch of usable tape. I have no set, thanks to Tommy's little surprise at the bar. And now I find I haven't got any actors either.

My entire cast of foreign students is far too busy filling out grant applications to devote any time to me.

Tommy's philosophy: "If you apply for everything, something's going to come through."

"Come on," I wheedle. "I only need a few hours. How long can it take to fill out forms?"

"Are you kidding?" he retorts. "Some of these guys from the really good countries, they've got fifty, sixty foundations to apply to. And it's not just forms. We're talking cover letters, essays, birth certificates, transcripts. I'm already out two hundred bucks of my own money just for photocopying."

What can I say to that? He's doing something legitimate, even noble.

Mr. Baumgartner puts a few extra nails in my coffin. "This project will be one hundred percent of your midterm grade." He looks meaningfully into our faces. "If you don't hand it in on time, I've got nothing to mark you on. I'll have to give you a zero for the first half of the semester."

That would be just peachy, for Anthony Luca to check on the status of his thirty-five-thousand-dollar investment and see a big goose egg beside my most important class.

I'm up every night brainstorming story ideas over the racket made by Trey, Tommy, and the uncles having their fried-chicken social. While three-hundred-dollar hotel rooms stand empty, these "tourists" prefer to pack into our tiny space to watch TV and play darts and Nerf basketball.

"We're not disturbing you, are we?" asks Tommy, the Shaquille O'Neal of the group, posting up Uncle No-Nose under the plastic hoop.

"Yes!" I snap angrily.

But I don't have the heart to make a big deal out of it. Not that I care about inconveniencing Tommy or the uncles. It's Trey I feel sorry for. His worst fears about Willow are coming true. She's basically dumping him, and the poor guy is despondent.

I try to cheer him up. "Who needs her, man? There are millions of girls in this town! You've got to make the city work for you! You said so yourself, remember?"

He looks haunted. "There's something about Willow. Every time I close my eyes, she's there. You don't know what it's like."

I know *exactly* what it's like. With Kendra giving me the cold shoulder, the image of Willow in that minidress has become the screen saver on both my retinas. She's called a couple of times, too, always when she knows Trey will be in class. So far, I've been pretty good at brushing her off. That's the only reason she hasn't got me wrapped around her little finger even more firmly than Trey.

"Try not to think about it," I advise. "The sooner

you get over her, the sooner you can find yourself another girlfriend."

"No way," he moans. "Tommy's right. The only way to handle this is to find the guy she ditched me for."

"What's the point?" I ask, since "the guy" is probably me. "What are you going to do? Punch him out? That's not going to make her take you back."

"But at least I'll *know*."

You see? He's not just miserable; he's totally bent on wallowing in it. The kid is the mood equivalent of MSG—all flavors enhanced. His roommate can't be just a friend; he has to be a lifelong till-death-do-us-part blood brother. L.A. can't be a nice place; it has to be the undisputed glittering epicenter of all that's good in the world. And when his girlfriend turns on him, it can't be just a bummer. He blows it up into a tragedy of apocalyptic proportions.

Now he's thrown himself into Nerf basketball in the same warped way. He dives for every loose ball like the NBA title is on the line, has screaming fits over fouls, and even conducts mock interviews. How can I put a stop to it? Playing stupid games with the invaders from New York has become the only thing that gives Trey enjoyment anymore.

Besides, what's the point? Even if I do come up with a decent idea for my video, I've got no actors. The foreign students are out, my classmates have their own projects to worry about, and the uncles sure aren't going to volunteer. They're wiseguys.

Basically, I'm caught. If I can't come up with actors, the greatest story in the world won't help me.

Where am I going to find a bunch of people who have nothing better to do than waste their time just to save my derriere?

I rap smartly on the door of the Lambda Chi house. A short blond kid answers, takes one look at who it is, and turns ghostly white.

"Vince! Long time, no see! Come on in!"

Several of the brothers are there to greet me, including old crazywags himself, Paul Waghorn, fraternity president.

"We were thrilled to get your call, Vince. Just tell us what you need us to do."

My actors.

Look, I'm not proud of this. I *never* use my position as a son of the Mob. But this is an emergency. I have to show this video *tomorrow*, or take that zero. And Tommy has these guys so spooked that not one of them would dare say no to me.

"The project is called 'Vignettes of Fraternity Life.' So all you have to do is act naturally. Go about your business. Do what you normally do around the frat house. I'll shoot it—you know, videotaping—" I add quickly, "and cut it together tonight."

Yes, I know it's really bad. Every twit without a shred of imagination ends up filming daily life in a dorm or apartment or house. But I'm in real trouble, perilously close to missing the deadline. It goes without saying that my project will stink. But at least it won't be nothing.

I give Waghorn a floodlight, and we go off to capture the essence of Lambda Chi.

Turns out, that essence is a bunch of frat boys walking around with hot pokers up their butts because they're so scared of me. They don't talk; they don't smile. One guy can't even brush his teeth when I stick the camera in his bathroom door. The place comes across like the Lambda Chi Funeral Home, with the brothers tapping each other decorously on the shoulders and speaking in muted tones.

I lower the camcorder. "Listen—this isn't working." They look petrified. "It's no big deal," I reassure them. "I just need a little more, you know, action."

Suddenly, it becomes frenetic. Loud music blares from every room. Guys shoot up and down the stairs with giant armloads of stuff. Papers fly. Everybody talks nonstop, except for the ones who are singing. Empty wine jugs and even small chairs are pitched out the upstairs windows into the backyard where the late Stedman once stood. One guy does cartwheels in the hall. Another is tightrope walking on the upstairs banister. But just as before, no one is smiling.

By the time I yell "Cut!" the place is a shambles, and the brothers of Lambda Chi look like they've been through a small war. They're sweaty, exhausted, wild-eyed, and still scared. They also have about two hours of cleanup ahead of them.

"That was—great," I manage. "I owe you."

"No, you don't!" exclaims Waghorn. "You're one of us now."

The thought depresses me even more than the quality of the footage I know I've got on tape.

I'm on the way out, practically free, when the door opens, and the vision that is Willow floats into the frat house.

She throws her arms around me. "Hey, stranger!"

In the space of that two-second encounter, I realize something: all my promises to myself that nothing is going to happen again between me and Willow are pure hot air. Because when I see her, I just plain want her. End of story.

If I succeed in keeping my hands off Trey's ex-girlfriend, it's not going to be a triumph of willpower. It's going to be because I manage to stay out of her way.

Even now, only the mess saves me.

"Jeez, guys," she exclaims in amazement. "What hit this place?"

A chorus of babbled explanations rises from the brothers.

And before she can turn back to me, I heft my camera and lighting gear, and run for my life.

With the project due tomorrow, I have to wait almost two hours for an editing booth in the video lab. When I finally do get my hands on the equipment, I realize the extent of the disaster.

My footage looks like a cross between *Animal House* and the sack of Rome. An Academy Award–winning editor couldn't make anything out of this junk. It's twenty-one minutes and sixteen seconds of—I don't even know how to describe it!

Desperately, I come up with a plan. I splice together a few minutes of the early part of my shoot, with the actors shuffling around like undertakers. Next, I take advantage of some stock footage that's available to us. It comes from a cheap old science fiction movie, an alien invasion of L.A. It's twelve seconds long, and shows a flying saucer parking itself in the air and enveloping a house below it in really hokey green light, supposedly some futuristic ray. Finally, I cut to the last part, with the crazed brothers scrambling around like chickens with their heads cut off, trashing their surroundings in a wild bacchanal of fevered panic. And I change the title, from *Vignettes of Fraternity Life* to *Metamorphosis*. Why not?

The one change I'd love to make is in the credits, where it says A VINCE LUCA PRODUCTION. This is definitely the kind of movie you show under an assumed name.

It all sounds pretty quick, but the truth is editing takes forever. It's four A.M. when I drag my finished masterpiece and myself up the bell-tower stairs to room 601. I toss the videotape on top of the TV, step over Tommy's sleeping form, and fall into bed fully dressed.

CHAPTER ELEVEN

INT. SEMINAR ROOM—DAY

The words "THE END" appear on the TV
monitor. *Metamorphosis* has just been
screened for the class. VINCE LUCA stands
at the front to accept the comments of
his peers.

> MR. BAUMGARTNER
> That is the worst project I've seen
> in all my years as a teacher. If
> you want a lesson in how not to
> shoot a video, this is it. . . .

> P-RICK
> God, Vince, how did you get into
> this department? Did your father
> threaten the admissions director?

I want a real man--a man who knows
how to make a movie. . . .

ANTHONY LUCA
Thirty-five grand for this? Do you
realize what happens to people who
give me this kind of value for my
money . . . ?

I awake with a start to a splitting headache and voices that have become far more familiar than they should have: Uncles No-Nose, Fingers, and Uncle, plus Gus, Rafael, and the Pope.

"Come on, guys," I moan. "What are you doing here at the crack of dawn?"

Then I catch a glimpse of the digital clock on my nightstand. It's 11:27.

"Holy—" I jump out of bed, and that's not just an expression. I literally fly, flinging the covers in all directions. TV production class started at ten! If I can't get there by noon, I'm dead!

"Why didn't my alarm go off?" I howl.

Tommy supplies the answer. "I shut it down. You got in pretty late last night, Vince. A kid your age needs his sleep."

I hurl a barrage of obscenities at him, words I didn't even realize I knew.

Tommy is amused and offended at the same time. "Let's go get some eggs," he says to the uncles. "Give potty-mouth a chance to go to school."

Luckily, I'm still dressed from yesterday. So except for the B.O. factor, I'm ready to roll. I splash water on my face, run my fingers through my hair, and grab my project from the top of the TV. My hand closes on an empty VHS sleeve.

I scream so loud that, upstairs, Anorexia stomps on the floor. *Metamorphosis* is gone!

I start to hyperventilate. It's 11:43, seventeen minutes to deadline! And I've got no project!

I'm gasping and wheezing, my vision literally darkening at the edges, when I spot it. The little cassette symbol is lit up on the face of the VCR, which means there's a tape inside.

"Those jerks!" I hit the eject button and stuff the tape into its sleeve. Bad enough they take over my dorm room and my life! But they've got the *gall* to watch my project without even asking.

I kick into my shoes and hit the hall running. I have no idea how many people I bounce off along the way. I just know that it's late and getting later, and that zero is on a collision course with my head.

As I sprint, my heart pounding in my ears, I reflect sourly that I already have a project that looks like it was finished at four A.M. on the night before the due date. Running in, unwashed and disheveled, in the last two minutes of class won't do much to dispel that image.

The Film and Television building is on the opposite corner of the campus from Louis B. Mayer Hall. So it's 11:56 before I finally barrel into my classroom, sucking air and holding *Metamorphosis* out to Mr. Baumgartner like a baton in a relay race.

He takes it, but he looks completely disgusted with me. "Thank goodness you left yourself plenty of time."

The class laughs.

The TV monitor shows a freeze-frame image of Kendra, wrapped in Bedouin robes, her mouth open wide enough to drive a camel through, belting out some sort of lament. On top of everything, I've managed to miss the sneak preview of *Burnt Offering*.

A dozen questions pop into my head, but all I have breath for is a pathetic rasped "Sorry!" as Mr. B ejects the old tape and pops mine into the VCR.

I collapse in a chair and wait for the opening shot of *Metamorphosis*—Waghorn, looking like he's facing a firing squad, mumbling, "Welcome to Lambda Chi."

Instead, the screen shows a large room, stacked with crates. The camera zooms in on a man sitting in a chair, kind of stiffly, I notice. Then I see why. He's tied to it. Rough hands reach from outside the frame and spin the guy around. He's got a gag in his mouth, but he looks strangely familiar. Almost like—

My heart does an honest-to-God backflip—

A Caucasian Yoda with heavy-rimmed glasses! This is Ellis Rank! How did he get on my video?

A man in a ski mask walks into the light, pulls a gun out of his jacket, and makes a very deliberate show of cocking back the hammer. Despite the muffled audio, that sound echoes in the classroom, where you could hear a pin drop.

"Take a good look at this face," intones a low voice that seems to wrap equal parts of indifference and malice into a haunting package. "Do the right thing, or you'll never see it again."

Maybe it's because I didn't get much sleep last night. But it takes until that threat before I clue in. This is not *Metamorphosis*, and Lambda Chi house is not going to appear in a few more seconds. This isn't even my tape! Somehow, my project got switched with an Ellis Rank kidnap cassette! This is the *uncles'* tape, proof positive that they're in this up to their necks. And I'm showing this felony evidence to my entire TV production class.

I'm already out of my seat, running for the VCR. I hit the eject button on the fly, and catch the tape as it pops out.

"I'll take the zero!" I gasp. Dad will have to understand about this one.

"But, Vince," Mr. Baumgartner protests, "don't be so hard on yourself! Sure, it's raw, but you can feel the energy and suppressed violence. I really *believe* the characters!"

So do I, Mr. Baumgartner, I think as I sprint out the door.

I had run all the way to the film building; I make it home in half the time. My heart is still doing calisthenics from the shock. But to be honest, the most awful part of this is the sheer *familiarity* of this predicament.

It's a vending-machine moment. No matter where I go, no matter what I do, the brick wall I run into is always my father's business.

The horror of it almost makes me ill. The uncles, Gus, Rafael, the Pope—those sick bastards hang around our room all night like dorm rats, eating chicken and playing Nerf basketball. And what's their day job? They're kidnappers, holding that poor union boss in fear of his life! God only knows what they did with his driver. He could be dead in a ditch somewhere, so add murder to the job description. What would Dad call that—multitasking?

I wonder which one of them was the video star in the ski mask. I try to place the voice. Was it Uncle Uncle's Queens accent? Or Rafael's South Shore twang? And the cameraman? For all I know, that was my own brother! He says he wants to go straight, but this wouldn't be the first time he's lied to me.

And who's the most depraved person of all? Not the perpetrators of this crime. It's their boss, who sits in his basement workshop, hammering together bad homemade furniture while others carry out his obscene orders.

Dear old Dad.

I'm walking in the door, but I execute an abrupt U-turn. Lack of sleep made me drowsy, but I'm wide-awake now. I head straight for the pay phone outside the pharmacy on the corner. My fingers are jackhammers as I dial the number, and wait for my father to answer his private cell phone.

"Yeah?"

"Write down this number," I order tersely.

"No, Vince, I'm not going to do that. I don't talk business with people I've got no business with."

I'm caught off guard, but I have to get through to him. "Dad—I know everything!"

He laughs. "Congratulations. You sure got the hang of this college thing pretty fast."

"You know what I mean—"

"This is going to save me thirty-five grand a year," he rambles on. "And if you come home right away, maybe I can get a refund on *this* year's tuition. I'm proud of you, son. Mom always said you were a halfwit, but I stuck up for you."

I slam down the receiver, feeling a rare pang of sympathy for Kendra's father. God help the FBI agent who's expecting Anthony Luca to incriminate himself over the phone.

If Dad refuses to talk about it, there's no way to change his mind. I'm on my own with this mess.

The room is empty when I get back. I'm pathetically grateful. I really can't face Tommy or the uncles. What would I do? Confront them? Yell at them? The way I feel right now, I'd probably end up bawling like a baby. After all the times I've rubbed against my father's business in the last eighteen years, you'd think I'd be a little less thin-skinned about it. The lawbreaking and sleaze doesn't surprise me anymore. But I'm always taken aback by how *vicious* it can be.

I look down at the cheap carpet. There sits *Metamorphosis*, the real one. They just tossed it aside like it was garbage. How perceptive of them.

I consider going back to the film building and trying to track down Mr. Baumgartner. Class is over, but it's still Friday, so he has to accept my video. I decide against it for one very good reason. He's going to want to know what that other tape was, and I don't want to tell him. The only good thing to come out of this rotten day is the fact that no one else recognized Ellis Rank on the screen.

I hear laughing voices on the staircase, followed by the jingling of a key ring. My decision is made in a split second. I have no idea what I should do, or even can do, about the kidnapped union leader. But the one advantage I have over my father's people is this: they don't know I know.

I stick the kidnap tape back into the VCR, and set the empty sleeve on top, just the way I found it.

Don't get me wrong. I'm not some crusading goody-goody, out to save the world. And I definitely don't think I've got the power to contain my father's criminal enterprises. Agent Bite-Me can't even do that with the resources of the entire FBI behind him.

But when you grow up with the clothes on your back, the roof over your head, even your college tuition financed by illegal activities, you have to do *something*.

"Hey, Vince, check it out!"

They come trooping into the room, and what a sight they are. These ruthless New York mobsters have all bought sombreros, each one gaudier, with more sequins and pompoms than the next. Uncle Uncle's has a flashing sign that alternates between KISS ME—I'M MEXICAN and BÉSAME—SOY MEXICANO.

Sitting on the head of the dullest man in Queens, it's hilarious, and I laugh out loud. But deep down I know there's nothing funny about these guys.

CHAPTER TWELVE

"REPRESENTATIVE SUTTER'S office." The voice on the phone is perky, almost chirpy. "How may I direct your call?"

"Uh—" For an instant, I'm tongue-tied. I want to do what I can to see that Ellis Rank comes out of this alive. But I'd hate to be the catalyst that sets in motion the chain of events ending with my father and brother going to jail. "Congressman Sutter, please."

"The Congressman is unavailable right now," she says briskly. "Who may I say is calling?"

Like I'm going to leave my name. The irony is that Trey's dad would probably take my call in a heartbeat. He'd assume his son boosted another barbecue and needed to be bailed out of jail. But I want this to be anonymous. The name Luca has to be left out of it.

"I have to talk to him," I plead. "It's really important."

The chirping begins to have an edge to it. "Sir, you'll have to leave your name, and someone will get back to you."

"But then it could be too late!" I blurt.

"Please leave your name and a number where you can be reached."

"I *know* Congressman Sutter," I persist. "He would want to hear this. It's about Ellis Rank."

"Sir—"

But I refuse to be cut off. "I saw a video. He's tied to a chair in a dark room, probably some kind of warehouse. And there are guys with guns holding him! I couldn't see their faces; they were wearing ski masks. I think—" I hesitate. I don't want to go too far, but I really have to make my point here. "I think they might be in the Mob."

I'm hoping to give up just enough to get Rank rescued, without landing my father's people in jail. With any luck, the uncles will have the brains to get out of there if they hear police sirens. Then again, we're talking about people who think brains are what you use to prop up your souvenir sombrero. I'm betting on their street sense being keener than their taste in headwear.

There's silence on the other end of the line. Finally, she says, "Sir, Representative Sutter isn't here. Nobody's here. I'm all by myself. I can't let you talk to anybody because I'm it. You're going to have to leave a number."

There's no way. My dorm phone also belongs to the congressman's son. My cell has a Long Island area code and a Luca surname. And I can't give him a pay phone and wait for hours or even days to be called back.

"I—can't."

She's almost kind. "There must be some way the Congressman's office can get in touch with you."

I have a flash of inspiration. "You can e-mail me. Write down this address: crazyvince@lambdachi.org." Let my fratboyhood be good for something.

"And you would be—Crazy Vince?" she prods.

"I'm a friend." I hang up.

The next thing I do is boot up my laptop. The university provides high-speed Internet connections to all the dorm rooms. I use my USM e-mail address a lot, but I've never bothered to check if crazyvince actually works. It would be just my luck if Congressman Sutter couldn't reach me.

To my relief, it's there. I enter the POP3 settings and get in with no problem.

I have thirty-six messages already. There's one from each of Lambda Chi's thirty-five current members, telling me how thrilled they are to welcome me to the brotherhood next spring. I don't know what Tommy said to those guys, but it must have been memorable.

The thirty-sixth is *The Greek Report*, an e-newsletter put together by all the fraternities on campus. The only mention of Lambda Chi is a brief obituary reporting the sad passing of Stedman, the presidential rubber-tree plant. The cause of death is listed as "freak lightning strike." There has not been a single raindrop in Santa Monica, California, since I arrived here a month and a half ago.

There's the sound of a key in the lock. I'm embarrassed, as if I've been caught surfing sex sites. I exit the e-mail program as Trey staggers into the room. He's got a pink souvenir-shop candle in his hands, shrink-wrapped, with the price still on it. That's how I know he's upset. When the merchandise he shoplifts is truly useless, it usually means my light-fingered roommate has issues.

He's white and drawn, and a little shaky. "I know who it is!"

"What are you talking about?"

He sets the candle down on his dresser. "The guy Willow dumped me for. I know who it is."

I experience a brief moment of panic. "Yeah?"

"I saw them. They were out behind the Dumpster in back of the food services building. I don't think they knew anyone was watching. And Vince"—he turns tragic eyes on me—"he's an old geezer!"

"Huh?" My relief that this isn't an attack aimed at me is immediately replaced by interest in this mystery boyfriend. "What do you mean by geezer? Like a grad student?"

"No, like an old guy. A middle-aged man with a bald spot!"

I laugh nervously. "Calm down. It's probably just her dad."

"No way, Vince! Who meets their father behind a Dumpster?"

He's right, of course. "One of the professors?"

He shrugs miserably. "Maybe. But it sure wasn't any student-teacher conference. Not out by the garbage."

I'm amazed by the flood of emotion that washes over me. I picture Willow, still gorgeous in spite of the multicolored splotches from incoming paintball fire. I hear her sarcastic commentary as we watch bad movies for the express purpose of making fun of them. I see her supermodel body sixty percent crammed into that minidress. And I feel her lips on mine at the Winkler Auditorium, briefly but deliciously, so soft. . . .

Oh, come on! I have a *girlfriend*—at least I'm pretty sure I still do. Willow Danziger should be nothing to me. In fact, I'm deliberately going out of my way to avoid a repeat of that kiss. Why should I care if she chooses to throw away her youth and beauty on some old coot?

"What does she see in him?" Trey laments. "He doesn't even have hair!"

"Maybe he's rich," I suggest.

"I don't think so," Trey mumbles. "He was wearing a polyester suit. I hate his guts."

I try not to sulk. "What are you going to do? It's her choice, even if it is the most brainless, crazy, stupid—"

Trey nods. "This is going to blow Tommy's mind. Your uncles too."

I'm suddenly down to earth with a crash. "What would you want to tell them for?"

"Because they'll know what to do," he says reasonably.

I'm not thrilled that Willow is messing around with some forty-five-year-old cheap suit. But no way can I allow Trey to tell Tommy and the uncles about it. Those guys really like Trey. For all I know, they might decide to do him a personal favor by dealing with this new boyfriend, vending-machine style.

I can't let that happen. I conjure up my most ferocious Luca Stare. "Listen up and listen good. You can never, *ever* tell Tommy and the others about Willow and this old guy."

He's mystified. "But we always talk over—"

"Never," I repeat, deepening the Stare. "You have to promise me, Trey, as your roommate and your future frat brother. If these things mean anything to you, we have to keep this a secret. Got it?"

He looks a little startled, but I think I got through to him. I'm so mild-mannered most of the time that when I go postal about something, it makes an impression.

"Yeah, sure, Vince. Whatever you say."

I check crazyvince religiously over the next few days, but there's nothing from Congressman Sutter or any of his people, just a few more nervous welcomes from the Lambda Chi's.

It's frustrating to waste time while a gun is

being held to a man's head. On the other hand, maybe Trey's dad is looking into my tip on his own. After all, I told his receptionist everything I know. It's not like the kidnap video gave an address or anything definite like that.

Representative Sutter continues to appear on TV, commenting on the missing union boss and his driver, and the upcoming concrete workers' election, which is only three weeks away. He says nothing to indicate that he knows any more than before. It's a little confusing, but the congressman might just be playing his cards close to the vest. All I can do is keep checking my e-mails and hope I did the right thing.

Believe it or not, I even have time on my hands now. Tommy has completely taken over my work-study job. Oh, I still have to go to the office, and I even answer the phone occasionally. But there's nothing to do, because every single foreign student in the department is filling out forms and applying for grants twenty-four/seven. I can just imagine Scooby's recent footage. If you think *Metamorphosis* is dumb, consider a long documentary about my brother at the photocopying machine, and Zora painstakingly dabbing white-out over her many spelling errors.

I'm thrilled. Think about it: if Tommy's

spending ninety-nine percent of his time with the foreign students, how can he be mixed up with the uncles in the Rank kidnapping? For now anyway, it looks like my brother really is turning his back on the family business.

The foreign students absolutely love him. To begin with, they're mostly in their early twenties, closer to Tommy's age than mine. They genuinely believe he's a genius, which makes them unique in this world. Although I have to admit that the way he searched out these grants and student aid foundations shows a savvy that most people don't have. I know for a fact that I never could have done it.

"Who would have thought that there's so much free money out there?" Tommy marvels, entering the latest submissions on the master chart, which takes up a whole wall of my room. Mitch the Bean Counter is an accounting major, and he says it's the most complicated and ingenious spreadsheet he's ever seen in his life. That's Tommy. His reading material comes from cereal boxes. Yet when something catches his interest, he can be sharper than an X-Acto knife.

It's proof positive that my brother is capable of a career beyond the rackets. But when I tell him he's got a real knack for accounting, his answer is: "What's a spreadsheet?"

"*This* is!" I point to his vast array of scribbled facts and figures, with its cross-references and running totals. "Whole companies run on accounting systems just like this."

He shrugs. "Who's accounting? If you're getting money, you've got to know who owes you how much, and when. That's business."

"But it's *any* business," I point out. "Not just Dad's."

He chuckles. "Guys back home, they spend their lives making score after score, but they never quite find the right angle. They'd swallow their tongues if they could see whole foundations set up just to give away money."

"For a good cause," I remind him. "To help students from their countries get a world-class education."

"Who cares what it's for? The point is, it's up for grabs. All you have to be is a foreign student, and we've got tons of those."

"And some of them are living on canned beans," I add. "You're doing a good thing here, Tommy."

A good thing, and not a small one either. According to the wall, Tommy and company have applied for over a thousand grants. These range in value from a few hundred dollars to help buy groceries all the way up to money for tuition and airline tickets.

Even Tommy admits that only a fraction of these has any chance of paying off. Still, if by a miracle, it all came through on the same day, Tommy's foreign students would be on the receiving end of $1,828,443.18.

My brother was never in a math class he didn't flunk. But I don't even consider rechecking that figure. I'm sure it's correct, right down to the eighteen cents. When you put dollar signs in front of the numbers, most mobsters turn into Ph.D.'s. Talk to Uncle No-Nose or Uncle Shank about percentages, and you get a blank stare. Ask either of those guys to work out a weekly vig, and he's a calculator.

So far, the only check that's come in is five hundred dollars for Cobi from the government of Mozambique's Ministry of Education. Not a great sum, but a great start, especially, as Tommy says, "for lying around, scratching your butt."

Calvin and Perry are so impressed by Tommy's spreadsheet that they're inspired to post a chart of their own. It's the Richard Starkey Sighting Log, tacked to the corkboard over the landing by the telescope. It includes such entries as:

10/14—false alarm—cleaning lady
10/17—false alarm—reflection in window
10/19—false alarm—brain damage

The last line is in handwriting suspiciously similar to Alitalia's.

I have to admit it's a little galling to see Tommy held up as some kind of role model. The foreign students in particular are so attached to him that they don't even notice me anymore. I might as well be part of the wallpaper. They discuss their hero in front of me like I'm not there. And the most amazing part? What they admire most about Tommy is not that he's helping them, not that he's clever or a take-charge guy. No, they think my brother's most endearing quality is that he's a "typical American." Tommy Luca! Obviously, everything they know about the United States comes from gangster movies.

They watch every move he makes with total admiration. Little things, like, Tommy never waits in line. He doesn't argue with people, he never pushes. He just goes to the front and acts like he belongs. And pretty soon he's walking through the door, with his disciples in tow.

Or traffic laws. He doesn't defy them; he simply ignores them. He drives at the speed that suits him, runs lights and stop signs, and parks where he pleases. If there's a hydrant there, then it must be in the wrong place. Sometimes he gets a ticket, but there's always a handy trash can to throw it in. To some of the students, those from authoritarian countries, this kind of careless courage makes my brother a kind of James Dean–like figure. But James Dean was self-destructive. Tommy's just being himself.

Rahim has this ancient Dodge Dart—I swear he doubles its blue-book value every time he fills the tank with gas. One day, he's parked in front of our dorm, but he can't find the keys. His spare set is back in his apartment, ten miles away. Enter Tommy, who, like Odysseus, "is skilled in all ways of contending."

He's in the car in about eight seconds, thanks to one of Zora's hairpins. The foreign students, Mitch, and Trey watch in mute wonder as he removes the cover from the ignition on the steering column. He carefully selects two wires, strips the ends, and touches them together. The car roars to unmuffled life, and the spectators break into worshipful applause.

Trey in particular is fascinated. He's climbed into the backseat so he can hang his head over Tommy's shoulder, taking in every detail of the operation. When the hot-wiring is complete, and the engine starts, the look on my roommate's face is sheer exhilaration.

"Not you too," I groan. "What is it about Tommy that makes everybody want to run out and form a fan club?"

Trey grins. "Well, you've got to admit it's pretty cool. It happens on TV all the time, but when do you get a chance to see it up close?"

That's because he grew up in a congressman's house. In my family, we get most of our cars that way. Every now and then the police come to grab some of our rolling stock and give it back to the people who really own it.

But it's good to see Trey smiling, even if it's only because he's watching my brother put on a clinic in grand theft auto. The roller coaster ride of my roommate's mood has been all downhill lately, although Willow's mysterious middle-aged boyfriend hasn't put in a repeat appearance since that first sighting behind the Dumpster.

"I can't get her out of my head," he laments. That night he shoplifts a Hanukkah menorah with a picture of the Jerusalem skyline.

"Oh, come on," I plead. "You're not even Jewish."

He's stubborn. "Unrequited love knows no religion."

"This isn't love. She's just hot, that's all."

But I've got nothing to say. I can't get Willow out of *my* head either. I blame P-Rick and his stupid video. If I could only spend some real time with Kendra, I wouldn't give a damn if Willow was dating Methuselah.

It happens to me more times than I can count: I'm in my room, grooving on my wraparound view. It's five minutes before dinner, I'm eating a Krispy Kreme doughnut, and my mother will never know. Life is good, right? All at once, a deep, sexy voice wafts in through the heating duct. It's Kendra in 801, rehearsing some number for *Burnt Offering*.

Bad enough I can't be with her—I have to have her dangled in front of me via the ventilation system. Worse, I'm listening to Kendra, but the image conjured up by my mind is always Willow.

My mind is a great photographer, and Willow is very photogenic.

So I've got Willow on the brain *and* Kendra on the brain. But mostly, I've got Ellis Rank on the brain. I still haven't heard from Trey's dad via crazyvince. I try concentrating on schoolwork, but even then I can't escape the plight of the kidnapped union boss.

Mr. Baumgartner is obsessed with my "project." "Vince, I only saw ten seconds of your video, but the passion and fire were remarkable for a first effort. It had a combination of cinema verité and film noir about it. And your actors! Who was the man tied to the chair? The dread! The suppressed fear! Where did you find him?"

Oh, if only I *could* find him!

I sigh. "Listen, Mr. Baumgartner, I can't show you the whole thing."

"But why?"

"I erased it," I lie. "It wasn't good enough, and I got mad at myself and taped *SpongeBob* over it. Like I said, I'm ready to take the zero."

He hits me with the compassion thing. "I'm giving you a B-plus for the first half of the semester. But you have to promise not to be so sensitive about your work. How can you develop as a filmmaker if no one ever gets a chance to see what you've done?"

My mind reels. B-plus. It's the highest grade I'm getting in anything. Although, technically, it's the uncles' work, not mine.

And a documentary, rather than fiction.

CHAPTER THIRTEEN

WHEN THE MESSAGE appears, it catches me completely off guard. I'm expecting the usual butt-kissing of Waghorn and the Lambda Chi's, when I see an e-mail from info.privacyblocker.usa. The subject: Urgent Meeting.

My stomach gives a major lurch. Congressman Sutter! Except for the Lambda Chi's, he's the only one who knows about the crazyvince address.

It reads:

> **We have to meet.**
> **Thursday night, 11 p.m.**
> **The beach at 101 Ocean.**
> **Come alone.**

It's unsigned.

There's no way to tell whether the message is from the congressman himself or one of his people. I can only hope that whoever it is knows how important this is. Thursday is three days away, and a lot can happen in that much time in my father's world.

I sweat out the next seventy-two hours as if a clock was ticking down to my own execution. It's a pretty big contrast to the gravy train of grant checks that now defines Tommy's life. Every after-noon, cheering foreign students show up at our dorm room, envelopes in hand, to watch my brother enter the latest windfalls on the wall chart.

Perry shakes his head sadly. "Trogs. It's an invasion. Like all you have to do is climb a couple of flights of stairs. These people don't care about our traditions."

"Not owning a toilet brush isn't a tradition," Alitalia points out.

I turn to Tommy. "Alex applied for his financial aid the summer before senior year, and didn't hear anything until Thanksgiving. How can these kids have money in their pockets so fast?"

"We didn't apply for the big-ticket scholar-ships," he replies. "Those guys'll crawl up your butt with a telescope. We concentrated on the dinky stuff: cash for food, rent, school supplies. You gotta pay that fast, if you don't want your people on the street. And it adds up."

Does it ever. On Wednesday night, Rahim's contribution puts the grand total over twenty thousand dollars.

Tommy is like the proud coach of a championship Little League team. He always has a big grin and an arm around somebody's shoulders. He insists on personally driving his acolytes to deposit their checks. Lately there are so many bank trips that on Thursday he trades in his rented Mustang for a Ford Expedition, because it seats seven.

I should be happy for them, but being around such nonstop celebration is exhausting. Maybe it's just nervousness over my upcoming meeting with Congressman Sutter.

My uneasiness comes from several different directions. First of all, tonight's the night I'll find out if I can prevent a murder—possibly two murders, depending on what's happened to Toothpick Anderson.

Second, it feels weird to be getting together with Trey's dad without telling Trey, especially since my roommate is so explosive when it comes to his father.

Finally, I'll be going all alone, in the dead of

night, to a deserted stretch of beach in a city I don't really know. I understand that a public figure can't be recognized at a secret meeting. But that doesn't make it any less creepy.

An unlikely combination of wiseguys, foreign students, and bell tower residents are embroiled in a Monopoly tournament when I slip out of the dorm on a "7-Eleven run."

It's only a ten-minute ride to the water. I park on Ocean Avenue at the top of the bluffs, and walk down the stairs to the Pacific Coast Highway at beach level.

Once I cross the road, the traffic noise begins to fade into the rhythmic pounding of the surf. It's a moonless night. The only light comes from PCH and 101 Ocean, the gleaming condo built right into the rock of the cliff.

I pace back and forth on the sand, playing with the loose thread of the Bad Shark logo on my shirt. Most of my Bad Sharks are falling apart like that. The stuff is as cheaply made as it is overpriced. I have one pair of shorts where the voluptuous mermaid is completely gone and even the title character has begun to unravel. Pretty soon all that's left will be that great white toothy leer, the Cheshire shark disappearing behind its carnivorous grin.

My thoughts are in a whirl, because I have

absolutely no idea what to expect. For all I know, Ellis Rank and his driver have been rescued already. But they could just as easily both be dead. Or maybe Trey's dad set up this meeting just to assure me that the search is ongoing.

Calm down, Vince.

I don't know how the congressman plans to arrive—by limousine? Helicopter? Speedboat? I assumed it would be some kind of grand entrance, but all I can see is a lone silhouette unhurriedly crossing PCH. A new thought occurs to me: how will Trey's dad react to finding his son's roommate waiting for him?

As the figure reaches the deserted bike path, I realize that he's too short, and his hair is too long. Representative Sutter has sent an aide for this meeting, just in case I turn out to be a crackpot. I'm disappointed, but it makes sense. Anyway, the important thing is to find out what's happening with Rank and his driver.

At about a hundred feet away I realize that the aide is a woman. I peer into the gloom as her features come into focus. Petite . . . slender . . . dark hair . . .

A split second before I realize who it is, I realize who it *isn't*. The sudden insight hits me like a physical blow. This *isn't* anybody from Trey's dad.

This has nothing to do with Congressman Sutter. He probably never even got my message.

Who, besides the Lambda Chi's, knows about the crazyvince e-mail address? The best friend and den mother to my future frat brothers.

She's coming at me in a postage-stamp tank top and a sarong slit up to the summit of K-2: Willow.

Now I know how the ancient Egyptians felt as they watched the Hyksos chariots thundering across the desert. Fear, fascination, resignation. The outcome is never in doubt in the face of such superior firepower, resist as I might.

I don't resist at all.

I would love to say that I tell her to get lost. That I think about Kendra, about Trey, about the old guy Willow's supposedly dating now. But she's too much for me, a force of attraction so far out of my league that logic is never a part of the debate.

We kind of fall into each other. Her mouth is tilted at exactly the right angle to meet mine. We're already locked together as we hit the sand. . . .

EXT. THE BEACH AT SANTA MONICA—NIGHT

Cue MUSIC

CLOSE-UP on VINCE and WILLOW, wrestling passionately . . .

```
. . . CUT TO . . .

EXTREME CLOSE-UP . . . ditto . . .

. . . CUT TO . . .

EXTREMELY EXTREME CLOSE-UP . . .
```

The universe consists of two square yards, and we're its sole inhabitants. I kiss her too hard, but I can't stop myself. The awkwardness doesn't seem to bother her. My clumsy gropes smooth into graceful caresses at the touch of soft skin over taut perfect musculature.

I feel as if I'm being played like an instrument. One moment her mouth is on my neck; all at once, my cheek is pressed up against her navel; moments later, our lips find each other again. Sorry, Kendra, but how can either of us expect to contend with such skill? I can no sooner stop than I can perform photosynthesis. Nothing less than an act of God could halt this runaway train. . . .

```
. . . CUT TO . . .

The WAVE, rolling in from the ocean.
The crest curls white as it comes
crashing ashore, breaking right over
the LOVERS. . . .
```

The jolt to the system is so total that my first thought is we've been struck by lightning. It's not a tsunami—it doesn't go on to flatten the city of Los Angeles. But it's big enough to wipe us out, drenching us with water.

We leap off the beach and each other, shrieking in cold and shock. People think of California as a hot climate, but the water off Santa Monica is just a hair warmer than glacial runoff. You know how they turn the hose on a pair of amorous dogs? That—on a cosmic level—is what happens to Willow and me.

We're standing there, dripping and shivering, covered in wet sand. She starts laughing. It *is* pretty funny—the mighty Pacific Ocean taking a potshot at our make-out spot. She says, "We can warm each other up—at my place."

How awesome is this girl? To take a hit like that and come up smiling. Yet a part of me knows it's now or never. One more look into those green eyes, and I'm lost for sure.

I just run. Childish, yes. Stupid, probably. Definitely rude. But it's the only escape.

"Vince—what's wrong?"

I don't even have the guts to turn around. "I'm sorry!"

Four thousand years ago, if Ammon-Ra had

sent a freak sandstorm to stop the Hyksos chariots, the Egyptian army would have had the brains to get the hell out of there. I make them my role model.

My drenched sneakers squish and slosh against the pavement of the Pacific Coast Highway, but I don't slow down.

CHAPTER FOURTEEN

BY THE TIME I get back to the dorm, the Monopoly tournament has reached a white-knuckle endgame. The neighbors and foreign students have left. It's Tommy against Uncle Uncle, with Trey cheering from the peanut gallery. They're digging in for what seems like a long night. Judging from the players' huge stacks of bills, and the paucity of the bank, those two guys are far too effective as thieves ever to go bankrupt. For wiseguys, Monopoly is an exercise in collecting two hundred dollars without passing Go.

"Whoa, look at you!" Tommy crows as I walk in.

I can only imagine my appearance, soggy and sand-encrusted, with the wild staring eyes of the hunted.

"I'm jumping in the shower."

Trey's incredulous. "You went to the *beach*?"

"'Everybody's going surfing,'" sings Uncle Uncle. "'Surfing, U.S.A.'"

"You went *swimming*?" Trey persists. "Man, I would've gone with you!"

Trey in a nutshell. How could I take on such a wild and crazy endeavor without my roommate?

"It was an accident," I try to explain. "I got hit by a wave—"

That catches Tommy's attention. "At 7-Eleven?"

"Did you get my Cheez Doodles?" puts in Uncle Uncle, replacing the houses on Boardwalk and Park Place with two red hotels.

"Hey, you didn't pay for those!" Tommy accuses.

"Sure I did!"

"Says who?"

I try to use this diversion to sneak into the bathroom, but I feel Trey's hand on my shoulder. "Wait—"

I turn to face him, but he spins me around again.

"Please let me take a shower—"

His face is chalk white. He releases me with a shove and storms out the door.

From the depths of the Monopoly board, Uncle Uncle smirks, "Hey, Romeo—unless they got piranhas around here, you're sporting a world-class hickey."

The hickey! The telltale half-moon bite mark Trey brought home on his neck after so many encounters with Willow. I must be wearing the same scar of battle.

"Trey!" I run after him, but the stairwell is deserted.

"The poor kid just got dumped by his girlfriend," Tommy calls. "He doesn't need to hear about your beach action."

"It *is* his girlfriend!" I'm so flustered and upset that I just blurt it out. "I was with Willow at the beach!"

It's tough to shock a wiseguy, but they stare at me.

"*You*'re the guy who's been messing with Willow?" Tommy exclaims.

"*No!*" I defend myself. "I don't know. We think there might be somebody else too. But she's been after me, Tommy. Stalking me almost. She tricked me onto that beach tonight. And then—" I shrug miserably. "I just blew it."

"You're telling me! People get whacked over what you just did!"

"Normal people don't get whacked," I lecture, "for any reason."

"Ever heard of crimes of passion? Stuff like this, it's a lose–lose all around. What if Trey comes back at you heavy? I gotta take care of it—that's what you do for family. Well, big-shot congressman's son; soon every cop in L.A.'s looking for me. Next thing you know, I'm spending the best years of my life in the can."

"Nobody's going to the can," I tell him. "Look, I hurt a friend. I have to live with it. But that's all."

"That kid loves you like family," Uncle Uncle puts in. "You two being roommates, he's always talking about how lucky that is."

A sarcastic reply dies on my lips. I never bought into Trey's philosophy of the mystical bond between roommates. Yet I can almost hear him saying it: *Roommates don't fool around with each other's girlfriends.*

A lot of extenuating circumstances led up to my presence on the beach tonight. Some of them might even lessen my guilt. But they don't change the fact that I'm guilty.

"Your chick went AWOL, and you're on the rebound," says Tommy. "I understand that. But this just isn't right."

It's the straw that breaks the camel's back. "You hypocrite!" I shout. "You *gangster!* What do you know about what's right? You've done bad stuff I can't even *pronounce*! Where do you get off preaching to me? Because you're out of The Life for a few weeks?"

Uncle Uncle goggles at my brother. "What?"

The scope of my blunder comes crashing down on me. In all of organized crime, no issue could be as sensitive as this. You can't resign from the vending machine business the way you quit the yearbook staff. People leave the Mob to sell out their friends to the cops—unless those friends find them first.

Wiseguys don't go straight. They go into one of two things: the witness protection program or the cemetery. Period. Someone like Tommy must know enough to send hundreds of people to jail. His "retirement" would have to be handled with the delicacy of a heart transplant. And I've just golfed the issue into the open with a three wood.

"Tommy—" I have absolutely no idea what to say. Should I apologize? Lie? Act like it's all a joke? The can of worms I've just opened goes far beyond Tommy or even Dad. This lies at the core of the entire Mob lifestyle.

"Tommy?" Uncle Uncle probes nervously. "What gives, Tom?"

My brother sears me with a Luca Stare as torrid as anything Dad has ever conjured up. For an instant, I'm afraid he might attack me physically. But instead he pulls his duffel from under my bed and begins to stuff his belongings inside.

"We gotta talk about this, Tommy," Uncle Uncle prods.

"We will," he promises. "As soon as I'm gone."

"I'm sorry!" In fact, I've never been so sorry in my life. I'm sorry for the Willow thing, sorry for belittling his efforts to go straight, and especially sorry for letting the cat out of the bag. "Please stay."

His reply is addressed to Uncle Uncle, not me. "I'm never coming here again."

It's the truth. That's the last time I ever see my brother in the bell tower of Louis B. Mayer Hall.

Kendra is upstairs in 801, rehearsing with P-Rick. Every note that wafts down through the vent makes me physically sick to my stomach. As a child of organized crime, I've spent a lot of time contemplating what does or doesn't make someone a bad person. I feel like I've crossed over to join my family on the dark side.

Sure, there's a big difference between racketeering and fooling around on your girlfriend. But I've forfeited the right to call myself one of the good guys. And as much as I want to believe it's the destiny of heredity, that's bull. If this was a video project, the credits would have to read: A MONUMENTAL SCREWUP BY VINCE LUCA. I did this all on my own.

INT. ROOM 801—NIGHT

Suddenly, KENDRA stops singing and falls into P-RICK's open arms, kissing him far more passionately than she ever did her no-good boyfriend.

> KENDRA
> I want you, Richard . . . I know you'll never cheat on me like Vince . . .

> P-RICK
> How long is this going to take? I've got an editing booth in forty-five minutes . . .

That's the one good thing about P-Rick. I can trust him to be too much of a loser to steal my girlfriend—no matter how much I may deserve it.

I'm praying Kendra doesn't stop by to say good night, but of course she does. When my lips touch hers I feel unclean, like I've been swimming in the Santa Monica Municipal Cesspool.

She's instantly on to me—FBI agent DNA,

remember? "Vince, are you okay? You seem really out of it."

"Yeah—I mean—I guess I'm just kind of wiped. Schoolwork and all that."

She gives me an apologetic smile. "I know it's been tough spending so much time apart. But *Burnt Offering* wraps next week. I promise we'll be together then. It'll be exactly like before—you'll see."

Hearing that, now of all times, is far crueler than if she just went ahead and dumped me. I feel lower than primordial slime.

Trey doesn't return at all that night. I know this because I'm not asleep for a nanosecond of it.

It's after dawn before I fall into an uneasy doze. When I do wake up, it's to the thump of a George Foreman grill being plopped unceremoniously on my roommate's desk.

I sit up, rubbing stinging eyes. "Where did you go last night?"

"I just walked around." He won't even glance in my direction. "I had some decisions to make. Like, if you touch my grill, you die. Understand? This grill is off-limits to you."

I want to crawl into a hole. Now I'm even beating myself up for things I have nothing to do with. Trey was a klepto long before he ever met me. But I feel like I stole that grill personally.

He looks terrible. His eyes are red and swollen from lack of sleep, and his hair and clothes are windblown. He's probably lucky to be alive. In times of stress, Trey likes to take long strolls through bad neighborhoods, as if tempting the Fates (and possibly the locals) to take a shot at him. It's part of the wallowing process.

"Listen, man, I'm sorry. It's just—" What can I say? She won't leave me alone? She can't keep her hands off me? It would only rub salt in his wounds.

It hits me: that's the *real* reason I want to talk to Trey, to make myself feel better. Selfish Vince all over again. "I'm just sorry."

"I'm cooking dinner tonight," he continues. "I'm making ahi tuna steaks. Only nonscumbags invited. I'm calling Tommy and your uncles. They'll appreciate gourmet fish on a gourmet grill. I hope you don't need a three-pronged plug for this thing."

He can't reach Tommy or the uncles, and he burns the fish, and short-circuits the grill. Later, I walk in on him eating Chinese food with Calvin and Mitch.

He's irrepressible. "Get out of here, Vince. This Chinese food is off-limits to you."

His anger at my betrayal does nothing to dampen his flare for the dramatic. He steals things just so he can ban me from touching them. And he delights in coming up with California-style consequences for what will happen if I do: "You'll be shaved bald, strapped into a convertible, and driven around L.A. until you get sunstroke."

I suck it up for a few days before trying again to explain myself. "It was a one-time thing, you know. I wasn't dating her behind your back, and I'm sure not dating her now. I wouldn't do that to a roommate."

"We're not roommates," he replies coolly. "We're just a couple of guys who got stuck in the same prison cell."

So much for the ultimate Angeleno in his smokin' town. When Trey sours, the entire metro area sours along with him.

I know he's stopped dropping by Lambda Chi house, because Paul Waghorn flags me down across a crowded Third Street Promenade to tell me so. The frat president practically flattens a dozen people to deliver the news.

"Yeah, I kind of figured," I sympathize. "Things didn't work out with him and Willow. He's avoiding you to avoid her."

He seems bewildered by this.

"You know," I explain, "because Willow is such a close friend of the frat."

The logic eludes him. "She only hung out with us because of you guys."

Huh? "She's practically a brother—or a sister—whatever you call it. And she used to date the old pledge chair—" He's blank. "No?"

"She just showed up on the afternoon of the Fall Fling Bash and volunteered to put up posters. When I saw her with Trey that night, I assumed she was helping him get a bid to pledge." He looks nervous. "*You're* still pledging, right Vince?"

"You know, you're probably okay without me. Tommy isn't really hanging around anymore. . . ." I don't have the heart to finish the thought. "I'm still pledging," I sigh.

It's a sad comment on the Greek system that the kid with the congressional pedigree is no longer the indispensable recruit. That honor now falls to the mobster's son with the crazy brother. The old order is changing—to the even *older* order.

Speaking of Tommy, I haven't seen him since Willow night. I know he's around though, because somebody broke into our room and stole the big spreadsheet from the wall. He also sends his representative, Zora, to the foreign student office every afternoon to pick up any checks that might arrive there.

"How's Tommy doing?" I ask her.

She slaps my face. "Tommy, he is *good* person! You are mean, very bad brother to him!"

The uncles have also been missing in action, which is to say they're back at their hotel, where they belong. As far as I'm concerned, that's a big plus, but I feel bad for Trey, who loves them. Think about it: he's lost his girlfriend, his roommate, his frat-brothers-to-be, and his late-night hanging-out buddies.

Adding to Trey's funk is the fact that the union election, scheduled for October twenty-ninth, is drawing near. Representative Sutter plans on supervising the vote counting personally. Once again, the congressman's earnest Republican features smile down from every magazine and TV newscast. Poor Trey's head must be spinning.

This city is definitely not working for him.

CHAPTER FIFTEEN

WHEN THE GOING gets rough, it's good to have a friend like Alex Tarkanian to remind you that things could be even worse.

"I can't talk here, Vince. I'll call you back on my cell."

Thirty seconds later, my phone rings. "How's life?" I greet him.

"What life?" he replies bitterly. "I have no life. I have Frankie."

"Still?" I'm horrified. "It's been almost two months! Isn't his place ready yet?"

He sounds miserable. "I don't know. I'm starting to think that he never had a real place. My closet is his place, and he *just won't leave*!"

"He doesn't have *any* plans for moving?"

"Oh, sure," he says. "He plans to move his butt

from the chair to the refrigerator. Then he's going to move it back again. That's the only kind of moving Frankie's got in mind. Remember I told you he doesn't take me out partying anymore? Well, now he doesn't go out, *period*."

"Come on!"

"Seriously! He hasn't left the room in two weeks. I've got a hermit sleeping in my closet. If I didn't sneak him cafeteria food, he'd starve. I'm afraid to go home for Thanksgiving."

"You're going to have to stand up to him, Alex. Tell him it's time to move on."

"Don't you think I've tried?" he wails. "I've dropped about five million hints. He just complains about the Salisbury steak."

"You have to be more forceful."

"I can't," he quavers. "Frankie's your brother's friend, remember? You have to help me, Vince. You got me into this mess."

"Whoa," I say pointedly. "You got yourself into this mess. I warned you not to get mixed up with this guy."

His voice is shaky. "College is a nightmare. I'm flunking all my courses. I try to study, but there's Frankie, sitting on my bed in his underwear, picking his teeth—"

"Calm down—"

"Talk to Tommy," he pleads. "He's the only one who can tell Frankie to buzz off. I'm *begging* you."

"Well . . ." I've scarcely got the heart to break it to him. "Here's the thing. Tommy and I had kind of a falling out."

"What about?"

"It doesn't matter what about. The point is he's gone. I haven't seen him in a week."

I can actually hear him deflating over the phone. "You're killing me, man. Do you know what it's like to live with a person who picks his teeth twenty-four hours a day?"

Yes, I'm responsible for Frankie, just because he's Tommy's friend. Bring it on, people! If there's any blame to be assigned, give it to Vince Luca. He probably did it anyway. Who was Jack the Ripper? Vince Luca. Who sank the *Titanic*? Ditto. Vince Luca assassinated the Archduke Franz Ferdinand, gave the Russians the bomb, and invented telemarketing. Every unsolved crime is the work of Vince Luca. Put the cuffs on him. He can take it. He likes it!

I grab my books and throw open the door . . . and slam it shut again.

The stairwell is full of people—very agitated people. I check the peephole. It's the entire foreign contingent of the film school of the University of Santa Monica. Tommy Luca's faithful.

Before I can twist the deadbolt, the door is kicked back in my face, and the crowd surges into my room. An octopus of arms reaches for me, and I'm slammed up against Trey's X Games poster. For an instant, I actually believe that Tommy has put out a contract on his own brother, and sent his zealots over to whack me.

Zora pushes through the mob. She shakes me, her fingernails tunneling into my triceps. "Where is money?"

"Well—" One thing about life post-Tommy is, I'm a little out of touch with the saga of the grant checks. "I guess some foundations are quicker than others, so you really never know—"

"*No!*" she roars, as Scooby tries to perform camcorder rhinoplasty on me. "The money that already comes! The money we *have!*"

I shrug. "Didn't you put it in the bank?"

"It's gone!" wails Rahim.

"You spent it already?"

"*No!!*"

A barrage of bank statements and checkbooks is shoved in my face. I move from paper to paper, my stomach tightening as the numbers fly by my eyes. Every account has a deduction showing a single check cashed on October 25, last Tuesday. The amounts exactly match the sum of the deposits directly above them, the grants from the various foreign student foundations. It's almost as if all the money that came in was only passing through.

I don't get it. Sure, banks make mistakes, but thirty-one times? "Well, what does Tommy say?"

"*Where* is Tommy?" Zora rages. "He is disappear!"

Hello.

This is not a large-scale bank error. Missing money. Tommy Luca. Connect the dots.

My brother never intended to give up being a mobster. All this time that he's been talking about getting out of The Life, he's been putting together a scam!

What an *idiot* I am! Some of the things I said— "doing something positive," "improving the lives of these guests in our country"—Tommy never cared about any of that. He got them money so he could *steal* it.

They're devastated. And who can blame them? Thirty-one kids from all corners of the globe, who busted their humps to come to America to learn to be filmmakers. Their savings spent on tuition and travel, they live in hovels, crummy apartments split with crowds of roommates. Along comes a friend, a streetwise New Yorker who wants to help. And he picks their pockets.

Yeah, they're mad. I look from face to fuming face. They're mad at *me*!

It hits me—they think I'm Tommy's partner! That *I* did this.

"Hey, wait—I don't have anything to do with it!"

"Without you, Tommy, he knows none of us," Cobi accuses. "You are his connection!"

"I'm his *stooge*!" I defend myself. "He *used* me, just like the rest of you guys!"

The tension is broken by a muffled sob. Zora is crying softly into her hands. Yes, we've all been used by Tommy. But Zora thought she was his girlfriend.

"How could I be such idiot stupid-head?" she sniffles.

"It's not your fault." I soothe.

"Who else the fault it can be?" she demands.

"It's not just you, Zora," says Rahim. "We all loved him. He conned everybody."

But the biggest con wasn't on the foreign students or even poor Zora. What could have possessed *me* to believe that Tommy might go straight? Me, of all people. I've been flim-flammed by the vending machine business a hundred times, but that doesn't keep dumb Vince from lining up for round one-oh-one.

Am I so desperate to believe my family isn't all bad that I'll swallow any cock-and-bull story? How pathetic is that?

The foreign students were right the first time. This *is* my fault, because I allowed it to happen.

And, as Honest Abe Luca has often said, *You screw something up, it's on you to make it right again.*

I touch Zora's chin. "Don't cry." And when she doesn't respond, I bark, *"Cut it out!"*

The sniffling stops.

"There's nothing to worry about," I announce.

Rahim's dark eyes flash resentfully. "That's easy for you to say. We have rent to pay, film stock to buy—"

"And you can do all that," I assure him, "because I'm going to find Tommy and get your money back."

They perk right up. After all, I'm positively brimming with confidence and purpose. There's just one snag:

I have absolutely no idea how I'm going to keep that promise.

CHAPTER SIXTEEN

Two problems:

1. Where is Tommy? He's basically disappeared, and . . .
2. Even if I do manage to track him down, how will I convince him to give the foreign students their money back?

There is no more daunting task than separating a mobster from cash. Have you ever gone to a diner or a Laundromat where they've got the first dollar bill ever spent there taped to the wall behind the cash register? That's how a wiseguy is about money. He might blow thousands in a single night gambling or womanizing or living high. But give it away? He'd sooner pry his own heart out with a shoehorn.

With the possible exception of God, there's only one person with the authority to order a made man to hand over money.

The boss.

From a pay phone, I leave this message on the voice mail of Dad's private cell: "I'm waiting by the phone, so call me as soon as you get this message." I hesitate. Knowing Anthony Luca, he'll leave me standing here forever just to teach me a lesson. So I add, "If you want to keep your son out of jail, you'd better get back to me." I don't burden him with any more details, like which of his sons I'm talking about.

Over the next little while, a few people use my pay phone, but the calls are short and don't tie up the line for long. In the end, I'm only pacing for a little over an hour. The instant I hear the ring, I leap for the receiver. "Dad?"

It's not Dad. "Hey, Vince, it's Carmine. How's school?"

Uncle Carmine, vice president of Brothers Vending Machines, Inc. and Anthony Luca's underboss.

"Where's my father?"

"Your old man's tied up for now." At least Dad and Ellis Rank have one thing in common. "I'm holding the fort. What can I do for you, kid?"

"I have to talk to him. Tell him it's about Tommy."

"We're hearing great things about your brother," Uncle Carmine says. "We're all proud of him."

I pounce on this. "Why? What great things?"

There's an uncomfortable pause then, "It's just an expression, Vince."

"It's *not* just an expression," I persist. "What are these great things you've been hearing? Name one great thing."

He hems and haws. "You know—this and that—"

"Give me a for instance."

He's caught. He can either jerk around the boss's son or break Dad's edict on keeping me out of the loop—the devil or the deep blue sea.

"It's nothing. Just some angle he's working out there. What do I know from details? We get our points, your old man's happy."

I hang up on him. Here's the proof—just in case I needed any more than the emptied bank accounts. So much for help from Dad. He's getting a cut of the profits off this scam. It's worse than a cruel scheme to steal money from poor students. This is business as usual, the same business that has fed me and clothed me since the day I was born.

I start for the Mazda, and before I know it, I'm

racing. Wheels spinning, I lurch into traffic. As I drive, the nuts and bolts of Tommy's con game begin to coalesce in my mind: my job at the film school . . . meeting the foreign students . . . learning about the grant foundations. No wonder he made sure to drive his acolytes to the bank personally. I picture him stealthily removing a single blank check from each pocketbook and knapsack. Next, he's on the road in his Ford Expedition, a pawnshop and check-cashing dive tour of Southern California. I'm amazed the phony signatures held up. You'd think people would be a little more careful. Some of those amounts are in the multiple thousands. It's just a guess, but tallying the numbers from those bank statements, I'd estimate that Tommy took the foreign students for more than fifty grand!

Stone is the posh West Hollywood hotel where the uncles are staying. It's a pretty happening place; I can tell because the Euro-doorman looks at my Mazda like I've just parked a hill of fresh manure in front of his gunmetal domain. Inside, it's so dark that I nearly wipe out on the granite steps. The only unshaved heads are on the women and (slowly, my eyes begin to adjust to the low light) a decidedly unhip resident of Howard Beach, Queens.

Uncle Uncle stands ramrod-straight in the middle of the lobby, an island of the nineteen-fifties surrounded by all that postmodern industrial decor. I'll bet the management thinks he's retro.

"Vince, what a surprise." He keeps glancing at his watch while he's talking to me. "What brings you to this neck of the woods?"

"Where's Tommy?" I demand.

He shrugs expansively. "Ever since you kicked him out—"

"He kicked himself out!"

Rafael and the Pope appear across the lobby. Uncle Uncle shakes his head urgently at them, and they melt into a bank of public phones.

"When's the last time you saw him?" I persist.

"I don't know, kid. I'm not his babysitter. He bunked with us a couple of nights and split. That's the truth."

Maybe so, but something fishy is definitely going on. As his New York colleagues emerge from the elevators, Uncle Uncle flashes them not-so-subtle signals to get lost. I peer through the fashionable gloom. Is Tommy here? No. Still, I wouldn't put it past these guys to hide him from me.

"Well, if you see him, tell him to call me." I storm out and pull the Mazda away from the door, to the immense relief of the Guardian of Coolness. But instead of wheeling onto the street, I cut through the line of taxis and limos and reverse to the delivery entrance. I shut off the engine and peer around the corner of the building.

One of the limos pulls up to the front, and the uncles get in. It's a little weird to picture these street thugs in a silver stretch, but it happens all the time. Back East, Brothers Vending Machines owns a couple of car services. The businesses are totally legit, except when there's a big meeting, and a fleet of thirty-foot Lincolns shows up bearing wiseguys from all over the tristate area. Mob minivans.

I put the Mazda in gear and jump into traffic after them. My first thought is that they'll lead me to Tommy, but then it strikes me: what if they're going to Ellis Rank?

My heart skips a beat, and I step on the gas. If I know where the union boss is being held, I won't need Congressman Sutter. I can just call the police tip line and give the address!

It's all I can do to keep from driving right up the stretch's tailpipe. Calm down, I tell myself. These guys are pros. They can see when they're being followed. I drop back a couple of car lengths.

I'm amped, not scared—not yet, anyway. But if

the uncles stop in front of some deserted building, what then? Do I follow them inside? Naturally, my dad's people would never intentionally harm me. But this is *kidnapping*. High crime means high stakes, with major jail time if things go sour. Nerves are frayed, tempers are short, guys are jumpy. Triggers get pulled by mistake.

I've been entangled in my father's affairs before, but there was never any danger of winding up *shot*.

The limo merges onto the freeway, which makes tailing a little easier; at least I don't have to worry about traffic lights. The uncles head west, then south, and exit at Los Angeles International Airport.

I follow, frowning in confusion. Who's taking a trip? None of them has a suitcase, or even a brief-case. What's going on?

The stretch pulls up to the terminal. Uncle No-Nose jumps out and rushes into the baggage claim area.

An airport police officer waves at me to move on. Doesn't it figure? A carload of kidnappers is free to hang out all day while the cops hassle an innocent kid.

I circle the loop, bullied by Super Shuttles and rent-a-car buses. There's the limo again, nothing happening. Then, just as I pass by, I catch a quick glimpse of Uncle No-Nose in the rearview mirror.

He's escorting somebody through the revolving doors. It's the last person I expect to see in California. Yet his presence here makes perfect sense.

It also provides the answer to a question I've been asking myself for weeks: how will I know when something is about to happen in the Ellis Rank affair?

Answer: when the boss arrives from New York.

The newcomer is Anthony Luca.

CHAPTER SEVENTEEN

BROODING.

I'm getting good at it. With Trey avoiding me, I have the room to myself these days. The best brooding is done in private.

Anthony Luca in L.A. That's huge. My father almost never goes on the road. It's a sign of power in his world. You come to the boss; he doesn't come to you. But it goes beyond that. Dad's a homebody. He likes his couch and his TV. He enjoys his woodworking, although he stinks at it. I was the most overprivileged kid in town, but I never got to go to Disney World, because Dad has a thing about hotel food. I'm not sure what his specific problem is. Maybe it's Mom's cooking. Once you've had the best, nothing else measures up.

Dad in town—and just in time for the union

election, too. That's no coincidence. Something big is going to happen. I don't know what. But I can't see the result of all this being any good.

It's the helplessness that bugs me the most. Can't stop Tommy; can't stop Dad. Even in the Trey disaster, it was Willow who really called the shots. I might as well be a Ping-Pong ball, a shell of thin plastic, smacked back and forth by the greater powers.

An insistent rapping at the door interrupts my reverie. I peer at the luminescent dial of my watch. It's after nine. Brooding is always purer in the dark.

Suddenly, light blazes in from the hall, and I squint at the figure silhouetted in the radiant rectangle of the doorway.

"Kendra!" Her visits are usually prefaced by a couple of hours of rehearsal wafting down via the duct system.

She pulls out a fistful of papers and flings them. "Don't talk to me! Not one word!"

I'm out of the bed now. "What's going on?"

"You lied to me! You said you didn't like her!" She wheels around and storms out.

"Who?" As I stagger after her, my foot comes down on the fallen papers. My legs slide out from under me, and I hit the floor hard. It's there, flat on my back, that I get a look at what she saw fit to

bounce off my nose: a sheaf of eight-by-ten glossy photographs.

To call it shock is an understatement. It's a full-body experience, stiffening my joints, curling my neck hair, accelerating my heartbeat. It's not that the black-and-white images are so unbelievable. I know it happened—I was *there*! Yet the sight of it, captured on film—oh, my God . . .

Willow and me on the beach.

"Don't go!" I shout. Although, in fairness, why shouldn't she? I can't deny this. A picture is worth a thousand words—or in this case, a stack of dictionaries.

I blunder after her, missing the top stair and tumbling all the way to the landing outside 501. She pauses just long enough to make sure I'm not dead, and keeps on moving.

"These pictures!" I blurt. "They're not the whole story! Honest!"

She turns and shoots sparks at me. "Tell me the story, Vince. Because they look like a pretty good story to me. They look like a story from the back room at the video store!"

"I stopped it! I said no!"

"That's what you call *no*?" She's on her way down again. "Remind me never to join your team on *Quiz Bowl*."

I catch up. "She tricked me! I thought she was going to be a congressman—"

"You said she was with Trey!"

"She *was!*" It must be from Mom's side, because Dad knows when to be a clam. But at times like this, I can't seem to help digging my grave with my mouth. "They broke up! I thought it was because of me, but then there was this old guy! Nobody can keep away from her! She's, like, super-natural—"

"Shut up!" she screams. "You have nothing to say that I want to hear! Do you know what it's like to have your *father* bring you pictures of your boyfriend cheating on you? God, I'm as mad at him as I am at *you!*"

A single factoid penetrates my thick skull. "Your dad is in L.A.?"

She tries to slap me, a halfhearted swipe that doesn't make much contact. She could take a few lessons from Zora on the Slovakian technique. They'd probably be fast friends. They've got something in common: queen-size grudges against the Luca brothers.

We're out of the bell tower now, at the elevator in the fourth-floor hallway. "I don't deserve this," she seethes. "Maybe I've been preoccupied in California, but this goes beyond anything."

My deepest fear is coming true. I'm losing the girlfriend I battled two families to keep. It's not a possibility, not one of Mr. Lai's probability permutations. It's real life, and it's happening *right now*! I should be begging and pleading, apologizing at the speed of light—

And what's uppermost in my mind?

"Did your dad come out to visit you, or is he here for his job?"

There was probably still a chance to save myself until I asked that question.

"Bastard—you don't even care!" The elevator arrives, and she gets in.

"That's not it—"

But I'm too late. The doors swallow her up.

I'm a single man.

I should be crying, but my brain won't stop whirring long enough for me to feel any pain. First Tommy, then the uncles, then Dad. Now Agent Bite-Me. New York must be empty!

Okay, Tommy's got his own scam going out here. I haven't forgotten that little entry on my to-do list. But Dad and the uncles are all here because the vending machine business is mixed up in California union politics. And Kendra's father is here because their business is his business.

As usual, the feds are being nice and thorough. They're not just watching the uncles; they've got me under surveillance too. How else would Agent Bite-Me get pictures of my encounter with Willow on the beach? Your tax dollars at work. Murderers and terrorists run free, but the feds are always Johnny-on-the-spot to destroy my love life. We can all sleep better knowing that homeland security is job one.

I feel a surge of anger. If I wasn't Anthony Luca's son, no way would G-men be taking pictures of me, on the beach or anywhere else. This is another case of my family costing me something important.

But my rage is empty. Willow is *my* screwup, not Dad's. I could have walked away as soon as I saw her that night. I can blame a lot on my father, but not this. Add Vince Luca to the long list of weak idiots who got caught cheating. There are sports gigastars and billionaires and even ex-presidents in that group. The distinguished company is little comfort.

Now it's time for me to suck even more, by aiding and abetting a known felon. I have to warn Dad that Agent Bite-Me is in town.

Chances are he already knows. Not much gets past Anthony Luca. But I owe him a heads-up. Mob boss, or not, he's my father.

I tackle the customary set of communications

obstacles. I'm sure he's staying at the same hotel as the uncles, but I'll never reach him there because they're all registered under Marlow or Harding or Turner. It doesn't surprise me that wiseguys use aliases, but why do they have to come from the passenger log of the *Mayflower*?

So I do the pay-phone thing. Uncle Carmine has Dad's private cell. The underboss will know how to reach Anthony Luca.

I'm in luck. I get through on the first try, and Carmine calls me back after only a few minutes.

He sounds annoyed. "We can't keep doing this, kid."

"Tell my father that his favorite future in-law is in town." Remembering that Uncle Carmine can be thick as a brick, I add, "Agent Bite-Me," just in case he thinks I'm talking about Zora's father in Bratislava. You can never be too specific. Not many mobsters join The Life because infrared astronomy didn't work out.

The one good thing about these pay-phone calls is they're short. Carmine promises to pass on the word, and I'm back at the dorm in a couple of minutes.

"Hold the elevator!" A burst of speed, and I thread the needle between the closing doors. There stands Trey, glaring at me.

"How's it going, *hombre*?" For some reason, I've found myself falling into his idiom lately.

He holds up a box of multicolored Hanukkah candles—for the menorah, no doubt. "Yeah, I know," I tell him. "They're off-limits to me."

But that's not what's on my roommate's mind. "It's so typical!" he announces as we exit the elevator and start up the bell-tower stairs. "Every time he wants to play family values, I have to perform like his trained monkey!"

The edict has just come down that Congressman Sutter expects his son to be present for the concrete workers' election tomorrow. At this very moment, the Hugo Boss is being cleaned and pressed. Trey has been warned not to touch it until the TV crews are unloading their camera equipment at union headquarters.

I let us into the room. "Why don't you just say no?" I suggest. "You know it's only going to make you miserable."

"Look who's talking," he says mildly. "The maestro of making people miserable."

At first, I think he sees them. But no, he's just stashing his books. He doesn't notice the FBI photographs sitting in plain sight on my desk.

In a semester full of dumb mistakes, this has to be the pinnacle. It would have taken about three seconds to hide those pictures. And in my hurry to warn Dad, I forgot.

I pull off my jacket and toss it nonchalantly over the photos. My aim is perfect, but the wind blows the top sheet off the pile. I watch in agony as it floats down, settling right at Trey's feet.

"What the—"

I have no clue what to expect at this point. Rage? Tears? If he pulls out a dead octopus and whacks me over the head with it, it won't surprise me.

"You took *pictures*?"

"No—"

"What is this, some kind of trophy to you? Are you going to frame it? Tell your New York buddies, 'Hey, look what I bagged in California'?"

"*I* didn't take it!" I defend myself. "How could I?"

"Yeah, you were too *busy*," he agrees bitterly. "Is this how film students get their jollies—shooting each other in action? Jeez, Vince, I knew you were a backstabber, but I never realized what a pervert you are!"

"*Shut up, Trey!*" I feel bad for the guy, but I have an abuse limit. "I didn't get anybody to take those pictures!"

"Yeah? Well, who took them, then?" he fires back.

I give him the most ridiculous answer of all: the truth.

"The FBI!"

He laughs in my face. "Sure it wasn't the CIA?"

I flip over the photograph. Stamped on the reverse of the glossy paper is a single word: EVIDENCE.

He stares at me.

"You're always complaining about your dad. Want to know how *my* dad makes his living?"

He's bewildered. "You said candy machines."

"That's just a cover! It's the *Mob!*"

His eyes bulge. "He's in the Mob?"

"He *is* the Mob! He's one of the most powerful bosses in New York! And Tommy and all those uncles you love so much—did you happen to notice they didn't come here straight from charm school?" I'm so used to fudging the details of the vending machine business that, once the truth is out, it's like the bursting of a dam. "The feds followed me to the beach because they were looking to find something on my dad. *That's* where the pictures come from. You talk about how terrible your father is. Ever wonder why I don't? Because when your father really *is* terrible, you have to keep your mouth shut! You can't talk about him even if you want to, because if you say the wrong thing, he could go to jail. So forgive me if I don't sympathize with the *shame* you feel over terrible William Sutter. Because, *hombre*, you don't know the meaning of the word!"

I slump back, emotionally drained. It was cathartic on the way out, but now I just feel stupid. I never tell *anybody* about Dad's business. Alex knows, but only because he figured it out on his own. And I *had* to spill my guts to Kendra to explain why I was avoiding her parents. Otherwise, I keep my mouth shut.

Poor Trey looks pretty rattled. It's a big concept to get your head around: that, for the past two months, you've been living with the Godfather's son, and all your new "buddies" are criminals.

"You're—" He backs away from me, unable to come up with the right adjective. Another step and he knocks over his desk chair, yelping in shock.

The guilt from the Willow thing is nothing compared with the feeling of having your roommate look at you with loathing and even fear in his eyes.

"Not me, Trey. My family."

But he's already scrambling out of the room, stumbling over the legs of the overturned chair. I spring onto the landing in time to see Calvin's telescope rocking on its stool as Trey hustles down past the fifth floor.

CHAPTER EIGHTEEN

WHEN TREY SUTTER is in this kind of mood, sooner or later, he's going to steal something. I've got to stop him.

He's already gone when I hit the lobby. "Which way did he go?" I bark at the usual suspects watching MTV in the lounge.

They don't even notice me, and the girl at the front desk just shrugs. I can either pick a direction and gamble, or opt for superior speed. I choose the second option and sprint for my Mazda.

I follow a pattern of steadily widening spirals from Mayer Hall. There's no sign of Trey. I'm amazed that he's out of range so quickly. He must be flying.

Switching tactics, I cruise up and down some

of the main drags. It's almost eleven, and the neighborhood is pretty empty. No way could I have missed him.

I swing by Home Depot and some of the other stores that have been Trey's shoplifting targets in the past. At last, I follow Lincoln Boulevard into Venice, where things tend to stay open later. Even here, the streets are deserted. L.A. isn't hopping like Manhattan. The nightlife tends to pool in little pockets spread around town.

The Lincoln Boulevard shops are mostly closed, even Bad Shark, Trey's five-finger Shangri-la. And—what's that? When I roll down the window, a low but persistent ringing gets a whole lot louder. A burglar alarm. But where is it coming from?

Then I see it: Vintage Collectibles, the classic auto place next door. I throw the Mazda into reverse and back up to the showroom. I notice the hole right away, the size of a cantaloupe, punched through the glass of the front door, just above the lock. The rear security gate has been opened to the alley. I can see that through the display window. But, as far as I can tell, nothing has been stolen. The cars are all in place, except—

My pulse drumrolls. The one missing vehicle is a certain old-fashioned Volkswagen bus painted in nineteen-sixties psychedelia.

My heart is pounding in time with the jack-hammer in my head. It's the shoplift to end all shoplifts—and the great granddaddy of monkey wrenches to throw into his father's plans. This is not the kind of thing the cops can chuckle and wink and shrug off, not even for Representative Sutter. I bet this was Trey's doomsday plan the whole time, his ultimate weapon to set off when the tide turned against him. I should have seen it coming way back when he spoke those fateful words: "I worship this car."

But who knew a small-time klepto like Trey could commit grand theft auto?

All at once I realize that *I* knew. My own brother taught him how to do it when he hot-wired Rahim's Dodge Dart. No wonder Trey watched with such fascination. It was *research*—a necessary skill, to be stored away for this very moment.

I wheel the Mazda around in a very illegal U-turn, narrowly missing a cruising convertible. I have no idea where he might be headed with the VW. But if the episode with the stolen barbecue is any indication, he *wants* to get caught. He might even drive the bus back to Santa Monica and park it right in front of our dorm.

My sneaker presses harder on the gas as I

approach the USM campus. The headlights come out of nowhere, and I'm suddenly blind. I stomp on the brakes so ferociously that the Mazda fishtails in a shriek of burning rubber. Centrifugal force plasters me against the door as I spin out of control, waiting for the explosion of metal on metal when I plow into the other car.

Miraculously, it doesn't happen. I lurch to a halt, intact. The "headlights" hover in front of the windshield, bobbing slightly. I squint into the glare. Four floodlights blaze on a handheld rig. At the center is mounted a small video camera. And behind it—

"Scooby!" I howl. "Are you crazy? What are you doing here?"

The blond Scandinavian rakes me with tragic blue eyes. "I shoot my beautiful city at night—while still I can."

I have no time for this, and definitely no patience. "What are you talking about?"

"My tuition installment, it is due, and I have not this money." Those startling eyes fill with tears. "If I am throw out of school, my student visa is revoke, and I am in Oslo in the New York minute."

Tommy. Every day is a reminder of what my last name is.

"Come on, Scooby," I plead. "I registered you.

You had enough to pay all your tuition. And Tommy only took the grant money, nothing more."

"Yes," he agrees. "But when the grant comes, I spend more. Live a little." He hangs his head in shame.

I make the decision in a split second. "Get in the car!" The search for Trey will have to wait. I'm going to take this poor Norwegian straight to Anthony Luca. There, we're going to rat Tommy out to his father and boss.

Okay, nobody likes a tattletale, especially not in the world of *omertà*, the code of silence. But I can't let Scooby get deported just because the USM film school's foreign student assistant happens to have a brother who's a crook. Only Dad has the power to squeeze that stolen money out of Tommy.

I head inland toward West Hollywood and the hotel. All the way there, Scooby sticks his head, shoulders, and lighting rig out the back window, filming I-10 as it races past.

"Put that damn thing away," I snap. "You want to get us pulled over?"

He finally agrees to lose the lights, but never stops filming.

With my foot heavy and the traffic light, we make it to West Hollywood in twenty minutes. There, our progress slows to a crawl, and it takes us just as long again before we pull into the palm-lined circular drive of Stone.

One look at Scooby, and the doorman starts grimly toward us. In a snooty place like this, the Palmcorder has "paparazzi" written all over it. That's a definite no-no.

But I can't think about that now, because I'm watching Uncle Uncle, Uncle No-Nose, Uncle Fingers, Gus the Greek, Rafael, the Pope, and Anthony Luca himself piling into their silver stretch Lincoln parked at the front entrance.

In a heartbeat, my focus shifts yet again. It's almost midnight, and I sincerely doubt that my father and his goons are going out clubbing. With the union election twelve hours away, this little nocturnal jaunt must have something to do with Ellis Rank.

Maybe they're going out clubbing after all. With real clubs.

I grimace. Not funny. Not even close.

I step on the gas, and the Mazda lurches forward, nearly tossing Scooby out the rear window. The angry doorman has to jump out of the way to avoid becoming my hood ornament. I weave around Beamers, Benzes, and Bentleys, and peel after Dad's limo.

Scooby is surprised. "Where do we go?"

"Sit tight," I grit. "And put away that camera!" I'm guessing Dad's opinion of video hasn't changed since the Aunt Palma debacle.

But Scooby films on as I tail Dad down Wilshire Boulevard. Jaw set, I don't take my eyes off that shiny Simonize-job. Wherever it's going, I intend to be right there.

The effort of staying in range takes such concentration that I almost miss it. Horn honking wildly, somebody is coming up on my right, driving like a maniac, half on the sidewalk. I stand my ground; I don't want to lose Dad. Besides, I'm a New Yorker.

But this guy's nuts. He pulls up beside me, swerving to avoid a fire hydrant. I swear he passes within half an inch of my passenger-side mirror.

"Veer off!" I shout. Although he really has no place to veer, except into telephone poles and buildings.

That's when I get a good look at the vehicle beside me. It's a multicolored Volkswagen bus from the nineteen-sixties. And unless there are two of those out tonight, the driver can only be—

"Trey!"

High up at the VW's enormous steering wheel, he doesn't notice me. Shifting awkwardly, he lurches ahead, cutting me off. I have no idea how I keep from ramming him. A poor schmoe in a Volvo, trying to pass me from the left, pulls in ahead, only to find the bus occupying his space. He swerves left again, sideswiping an SUV in a shower of sparks.

Trey blasts through the yellow light, leaving me mired in the snarl as the two angry drivers get out to inspect the damage. Instead of yelling at each other, they're yelling at the Mazda—at Scooby, who has the whole accident on video. Each believes the tape will prove that the other guy was at fault.

By the time I maneuver through the obstacle course of stopped cars and enraged motorists, Dad's limo is long gone, and the bus is a Day-Glo speck many blocks ahead.

I have no choice but to switch objectives yet again. I take off after Trey.

With the traffic stalled at the bottleneck, I have the street all to myself, and I catch up pretty quickly. I'm just about to roll down my window to scream for his attention when I look ahead. There's the stretch, right in front of me.

I drop back a couple of car lengths, falling into line behind Trey. It's there, tailing both of them, that I make a startling discovery. The stretch turns left; so does Trey. Then it pulls onto the free-way; Trey follows. And when it exits at Vernon, so does Trey.

Why is Trey Sutter following Anthony Luca?

My head spins. In a night of crazy twists, this has to be the craziest of all. Could my roommate actually be looking for confirmation that my father is who I say he is? Could Trey be so warped that he'd actually get involved with the Mob? And how did he even identify Dad? I rack my brain, try-ing to remember if the uncles ever mentioned their hotel to Trey. They were chummy, but wiseguys are notoriously closemouthed about details like that.

Yet what other connection could there be between Trey and Dad? Unless my father has had Trey keeping an eye on me since day one, and they know each other that way. Not impossible, but a pretty paranoid thought.

The limo wheels around a sharp turn onto an unlit street lined with seedy-looking warehouse buildings. My heart begins to race. If Ellis Rank isn't in a place like this, he isn't anywhere!

Ahead of me, Trey takes the corner on two wheels, but then suddenly slows in a screech of stressed gears. The forty-year-old motor stalls with a cough, and the bus shudders to a halt. As I approach from behind, he's trying to start up again. And I can tell from my Mazda experience that he's flooding the engine.

Dilemma number nine hundred of the evening: do I stop to rescue Trey, or do I stick with Dad? The answer is academic. The VW will be fine in ten or fifteen minutes. In that same time, however, seven mobsters can do a lot of damage to a kidnapped union boss.

I finesse around the bus, listening to Trey's muffled cursing. He still doesn't notice me, wrapped up as he is in his car trouble. For a minute, I'm afraid I've lost the limo. But there it is, four blocks away, at the end of the drive, parked in front of a two-story brick structure with boarded-up windows. I see a sliver of light: the door. Shadowy figures cross the narrow band. Then—darkness.

I don't even hesitate. That just shows how stupid I am. In my mind, the decision was made a long time ago to do what I can—probably not much—for Ellis Rank and his driver. God only knows why. Maybe it's human concern for those two poor people. Maybe it's a strange compulsion to try to reduce my father's lifetime total of sins by one. Or maybe it's just the simple fact that not a single thing has gone right for me since I left New

York, and I need an accomplishment to prove to myself that I'm worth the toilet paper it takes to wipe my butt.

I cut the lights and ease up to the curb behind a huge unpruned hedge. I turn around to Scooby in the backseat. "If you leave this car, I'll kill you myself." As I head toward the warehouse, I note in annoyance that the Palmcorder is now trained on me.

The sign says SHIBLEY TEXTILES. The paint is peeling, and it's pretty obvious the building has been abandoned for a long time. There's only one door. The knob has been removed, and I peer into the hole, half expecting to see an eye glaring back at me. But the coast is clear.

Gingerly, I open the door and slip inside. The place is lit up like a stadium, ready for night baseball. I wonder if the power company knows about this. On the other hand, if you're in the habit of kidnapping people, stealing electricity is small potatoes.

I think I know why Shibley Textiles went out of business. The place is nothing but long claustrophobic corridors leading to nowhere. Half their employees probably got lost and were never heard from again. In five minutes I have no idea where I am. In fact, I'm only aware of one thing: someone is following me, shadowing my every step in this rabbit warren.

I'm scared witless, but not quite so witless as to forget that this is all my own fault. This cinder-block labyrinth is full of gangsters and union goons. The chance that my pursuer is friendly is slim to none. I can only hope to be recognized as Anthony Luca's son before any serious damage is inflicted on me.

Another complication: there's nowhere to hide in this place. Not even so much as a broom closet. The one thing in my favor is, if I'm a sitting duck, then so is the guy who's following me.

So I park myself behind a blind corner, take out my car keys, and arrange them between the fingers of my right fist. Do-it-yourself brass knuckles, Tommy calls it. I don't relish the idea of taking advice from my brother, but there's nobody I'd rather have beside me in a street fight. I wish he was here now.

The approach of those footsteps on the cement floor chills my blood to liquid nitrogen. I steel myself, ready to spring. I can see his shadow on the concrete wall. Breathing a silent prayer, I throw a punch just as the figure comes around the bend.

My do-it-yourself brass knuckles freeze in

midair, half an inch from a Palmcorder.

"Scooby, you idiot!" I hiss. Not to scream at this imbecile is a trial of self-control. The fact that the building is full of gangsters is a contributing factor too.

"Vince—" he begins.

I clap a hand over his mouth. "Shhhh!" He's trying to tell me something, but now is not the time. His message soon becomes clear as a bell.

There's a loud cracking noise—the sound of wood splintering. With a reverberating crunch, an old broken window frame disintegrates, and pieces of smashed plywood and shards of glass come raining down. A second later, men with guns are pounding along the corridor toward us. Not just any men—*Luca* men!

Wait a minute! If these guys are just arriving *now*, then who did I follow? Who was in that limo Trey was tailing, the people who got here ten minutes ago?

I recognize Gus in the lead. More to the point, he recognizes me.

"Vince?"

At the sound of my name, Anthony Luca bulls his way through the running pack of uncles. They stare at him, amazed. Clearly, the boss's place is at the back of this stampede, not the front. Eyes bulging, my father leaves his feet like a linebacker and flies parallel to the floor, straight at me. He connects just above the waist, knocking me over and landing directly on top of me. I'm completely covered by a two-hundred-pound blanket.

"Dad!" I sputter. "What are you—?"

That's when the shooting starts. Instantly, two more bodies pile on, protecting their boss. Now I know the sound a bullet makes when it whizzes by you. It whines, like a jet-propelled mosquito.

I've been afraid before, but this is a sharper, rawer sensation, like a dentist's drill with no Novocain. It has a temperature too—cold, although the warehouse is stuffy. I feel consciousness slipping away as seven hundred pounds of beef gristle press down on me, turning my breathing into staccato sucks for air.

And the last sight I remember as inkblots distort my vision is Scooby's chalk-white face as he presses himself even flatter to the floor than I am.

CHAPTER NINETEEN

THE NEXT THING I know, someone says, "It's over."

The crushing weight is lifted from my chest, and I start to breathe again.

"Over?" I sit up and blink. Dad is hunkered down with Uncle Uncle whispering in one ear, and Uncle No-Nose in the other: the general being briefed by his staff.

To me, "over" can mean only one thing. "You did it. You killed Ellis Rank."

"This is none of your business," my father snaps.

"I made it my business!" I shoot right back. "What do you think I'm doing here? This isn't my idea of a fun place to hang out, you know!"

I failed. Not that I had much chance of succeeding, but it still hurts. I never met the union leader except on video. Yet now that he's gone, it's like I've lost a close friend. It seems worse than murder to me, the powerlessness of being executed while you're tied to a chair. This isn't the first time that I've had to juggle love for my father with disgust for his deeds. But never before has the contrast been so sickeningly stark.

"You're not human!" The words are out before I can stuff them back down my throat. "How can you sleep at night?"

"Hey!" says Uncle Uncle sharply. "Show some respect!"

"Let him talk," orders Anthony Luca. "You have to listen to Vince because he knows so much more than the rest of us."

"I know the difference between right and wrong!" I rant. "Is this some sick kind of fun for you? The big boss getting down in the trenches with his grunts? Is that why you showed up in person for this dirty job?"

It goes on. As a matter of fact, it gets worse. I unload on my father with both barrels. I'm so absorbed in my diatribe that it takes me a moment to recognize the man Rafael is escorting down the corridor. He's a little shaky, a little thinner, and he's lost his glasses. But there's no question about it—this is the Caucasian Yoda.

Ellis Rank, not dead at all.

He and my father embrace in the manner of two old friends.

"I expected the cavalry," jokes Rank, "but not the old warhorse himself."

"You lost weight," my father responds. "Maybe we should tie you up for a few more weeks."

As the uncles guffaw at their boss's wit, it all becomes clear to me. Yes, Anthony Luca is mixed up with the union, I was right about that. *But he's on Ellis Rank's side.* The Lucas aren't here to assassinate Rank; they're here to *rescue* him!

I'm blown away. "You mean you're the good guys? You caught the kidnappers and turned them over to the police?"

My father smiles with mock patience. "The cops don't do my job, and I don't do theirs."

"Yeah, but you can't just let them *go*." I stare in horror. "You *killed* them?"

Dad turns furious eyes on me. "The things you've seen here tonight—aren't they enough to prove that you know less than nothing? There are fire hydrants out there that understand more than you. A few bullets don't mean anybody's dead. Shots are like words, only louder. What we did tonight was tell some people it was time to hang it up and go home. That's all."

If I'm following his Mob-speak correctly, he's saying that once Ellis Rank is safe, nobody cares what crime was committed here. "And the kidnappers just get away with it?"

"Oh, right." My father's voice drips with sarcasm. "The cops won't want to talk to Ellis when he shows up after all these weeks. It'll never occur to them to ask questions like 'Who kidnapped you?'" He turns to the union boss. "My younger son. Goes to university out here. His mother spoils him."

"But who was it?" I persist. "If the Lucas weren't the kidnappers, who were?"

At that moment, a half-demented scream from out on the street rings through the shattered window.

"Da-a-a-ad!!"

Who said that? That's *my* line.

I run to the opening. Outside of Shibley Textiles are two identical silver stretches, one Mazda Protegé, and one Volkswagen bus from Vintage Collectibles.

Trey. So the flooded engine has unflooded itself. But why is he yelling *Dad*?

Then—a voice so often heard on CNN: *"Trey?* Is that you?"

"Congressman Sutter?" I blurt. What's *he* doing here?

I look up, and my father is smiling at me, the angry, righteous grin of an accused man who has been proven innocent.

I feel the deep shock of someone whose concept of reality has been turned completely upside down. Representative Sutter's interest in the union election never had anything to do with a desire to help his constituents. It wasn't even, as Trey thought, a cynical grab for publicity. No, the famous, respected, noble William Sutter was part of the conspiracy to kidnap Ellis Rank and hijack the union.

Trey's dad, the public servant, is nothing but a crook. And my dad, the crook, turns out to be the hero.

It makes sense. Trey wasn't following *my* dad; he was following his own. And anyway, both limos turned out to be going to the same place.

The congressman is with none other than candidate Pat McCracken and a couple of henchmen, hurrying to their stretch. But Sutter has stopped dead at the sight of his son at the wheel of the hippie-mobile.

"Where'd you get that car? What are you doing?"

The answer is the revving of a poorly tuned

SOUTH BURLINGTON COMM. LIBRARY
540 Dorset Street
South Burlington, VT 05403

engine. Trey's head hangs out the driver's window. "Hey, Dad!" he roars. "Let's see you explain *this* on *Good Morning America*!"

With a screech of the clutch, he shifts into first and stomps on the gas. The VW jolts forward, hiccups, backfires, and plows into an ancient sycamore. The metal front crumples; the windshield shatters. One tire blows, and the vehicle sinks off-balance amid the weeds. And there's my roommate, in a cloud of steam, looking out at his father in stiff-jawed defiance.

Beside me at the window opening, my dad whistles. "And I thought *I* had a rotten kid."

It's classic Trey. In his deranged logic, it's even brilliant. No way will Representative Sutter enjoy the limelight of page one, because on page two, his son and heir has stolen a vintage car and deliberately wrecked it.

The only problem is, nobody told Trey that the game has now changed, thanks to what just happened inside Shibley Textiles. Ellis Rank is alive, and with him survives the story that the distinguished gentleman from California is a felon. All the charm and gravitas and connections in the world can't get Trey's dad out of this one.

That new reality is not lost on Congressman Sutter himself. As his associates are pulling him into the Lincoln, he's shouting, "I'm sorry, Trey! I can't help you with this! I screwed up, and you're going to hear a lot of bad things—"

The car door slams and the stretch squeals off into the night.

I don't know what Trey was expecting from his father, but obviously that wasn't it. This is the first time the congressman hasn't been able to wave his magic wand and smooth over his son's shenanigans. My roommate looks stunned, bewildered. Most of all, he looks like he wishes he could replay the last fifteen seconds of his life. Before, he was in a position to drive that bus back to the showroom and have nothing more than a broken window on his conscience. But this is something that can't be undone with a note of apology and a few bucks for glass replacement. In less than eight hours, Vintage Collectibles is going to open up, minus one car. The call to the cops will come ten seconds after that.

I feel so bad for the guy. He's totally screwed himself. Even if he had a spare zillion dollars to fix a car that's been discontinued for four decades, where's he going to find an auto-body place at one o'clock in the morning? When garages like that work in the middle of the night, everybody knows they're chop shops, run by the . . .

I turn to Dad so suddenly that the cracking of my neck echoes throughout the warehouse.

He reads my mind in both content and nuance. "You've got some set of stones! Twenty minutes ago, his father's apes were shooting at us!"

"He's not his father, Dad," I plead. "They don't even get along. He's a good kid. And you're the only one who can save him!"

He scowls at me. "I'm also the only one who can dye my own chest hair pink, but I'm not going to do it. You're asking me for favors? Me? How many kinds of bastard did you call me tonight?"

"Don't take that out on Trey," I wheedle. "If anybody needs a break, he does. The guy's having a terrible year, and it's just going to get worse! What happens to him when his father goes to jail?"

Anthony Luca's cold hard eyes soften instantly, and I realize I've hit a nerve. I'm genuinely fascinated, and not just for Trey's sake. No force on this earth moves Dad when his mind is made up. But right now, something has given him pause.

I'm pretty sure I know what it is. When I was six, Uncle Bignose had to "go away for a while," which is what they tell you when somebody does time. My father was vigilant, almost maniacal, in making sure the family was taken care of. It's his biggest fear—his only fear, really. Not jail itself, but the suffering of your family while you're in the can.

Trey will never know it, but of all the times he's benefited from being Congressman Sutter's son, this may be the most significant.

"Okay," Dad says finally. "I'll make some calls." He holds out his hand, and a cell phone is immediately slapped into it. "I'm not guaranteeing anything. This isn't my turf. I just happen to know a couple of people who know a couple of people."

About a minute into the first conversation, I can tell it's all set up. Nobody says no to Anthony Luca, not even three thousand miles from New York.

When he gets off the phone, his first orders are for me. "Take your friend Jeff Gordon home and do *nothing* until you hear from me. Understand? You don't go out; you don't make phone calls. If the dorm is on fire, you stay put."

I couldn't be more eager to comply if his words were coming over the Emergency Broadcast System.

I turn to face him before I go. "Thanks, Dad. I'm never going to forget this."

"You'll forget it," he assures me. "By next week, this'll be something that happened to the Babylonians."

Trey is still at the wheel of the VW, deflated and

bewildered. All his adrenaline has been used up. It's like he's sleeping with his eyes open. He's unhurt, but limp as a rag.

It's an easy task to take his arm and lead him to the Mazda. "Let's go," I say gently. "I'll explain on the way home."

I'm surprised to find Scooby cowering on the floor of the backseat. To be honest, I totally forgot about him. If he was hiding behind a bush instead of in my car, I'd probably leave without him.

He's half out of his mind with terror.

"Don't worry," I reassure him. "Those were the good guys." I don't ask myself why the Luca family and the union boss are so tight. That's a different question, and belongs in a place I have no intention of going. Good guys or not, there's no way the connection is legal. Dad in a shady deal—been there, done that.

By the time we reach the city limits of Santa Monica, tears are streaming down my cheeks, and I can hardly see to drive. Crowded out by so many other revelations, the real top story of tonight is just beginning to sink in.

My father was willing to take a bullet for me.

CHAPTER TWENTY

UNCLE UNCLE IS ALL smiles when he shows up in the morning.

"It's done," he assures Trey and me.

"The car?"

"Not a scratch. Showroom door's even fixed. The whole thing never happened."

I feel like kissing him. "Thanks, Uncle." Dad's people come across like a bad comedy routine most of the time. I have to remind myself that he trusts these guys with his life. And Anthony Luca is no dummy.

"What about my father?" inquires Trey, subdued and red-eyed from a sleepless night.

"That part still happened," Uncle Uncle replies. "Sorry, kid. It's just business."

"When's Dad coming by?" I ask.

"He's already on a plane home," is the reply.

"He never hangs around for long. Hotel food gives him diarrhea."

Another great mystery revealed.

"I'm leaving too," he continues. "I've done everything they got out here: the beach, the tour of stars' homes, the tar pits—"

"You've made the city work for you," I add.

Trey doesn't even crack a smile.

I escort my "uncle" down to the fourth-floor elevator. "Listen," I say sheepishly, "from the very beginning I assumed the worst about you and the others. It never even crossed my mind that you'd turn out to be on the right side of all this."

He's gracious. "Right side, wrong side. We're just working stiffs, trying to make a buck, same as those suits over on Wall Street. The main thing is we got Ellis back safe."

I nod. "But what about his driver? Did you ever find Toothpick Anderson?"

"Not yet, but we will," he vows. "Can you believe that rat scum? Ellis was like a father to him."

I'm shocked. "Are you saying Toothpick sold him out? I thought he was a victim too."

He looks guilty. I can tell he assumed I already knew.

"You're going after him, aren't you?" I accuse him. "That's why you're leaving L.A.!" I shake my head. "You guys are a piece of work. You can do something so positive, and then follow it up by going after a poor little guy."

"Poor little guys don't dime on their friends and then run and hide."

"So turn him over to the police," I persist. "That's justice. Not ganging up on some skinny defenseless creep named Toothpick."

He looks startled, then bursts out laughing. "You crack me up, kid. They don't call him Toothpick 'cause he's skinny; they call him Toothpick 'cause he's always picking his teeth!"

Oh, God.

I look into my crystal ball, and the future appears out of the mist. I see a Mazda Protegé driving on a long highway. I see cactus plants on either side of the road.

I'm going to Las Vegas.

Ellis Rank is reelected president of the Southern California Concrete Workers Union. Representative William Sutter is conspicuously absent from the voting he agreed to oversee. There are rumors that he might be arrested as a conspirator in the Rank kidnapping. People can hardly believe their ears. To me, it's yesterday's news.

I hear all this over the radio in my Mazda as I

fly across the desert along I-15. So much has happened in the last couple of months that my head won't stop spinning long enough for me to think. But a five-hour car ride is a golden opportunity to sort things out. Like what a coincidence it is that the sons of the two men on opposite sides of the struggle to control the union should end up college roommates. Or the possibility that it's no coincidence at all.

Could Dad have manipulated my dorm placement to give the uncles a chance to snoop on Congressman Sutter via Trey? A plan like that could only come from a mind so devious, so cunning, so ruthless, yet also gifted with the foresight of a chess master—

Sound like anybody we know?

I'm not even going to ask him. First off, he'd never admit it. And second, I already know the answer. There are more than twenty thousand students at the University of Santa Monica. Trey and I, roommates by the luck of the draw? If you swallow that, then you'll believe the sign that once again sits on the roof of the nineteen-sixties Volkswagen bus at Vintage Collectibles: MINT CONDITION—ALL ORIGINAL PARTS.

Considering I've only been to Vegas once before, I find UNLV and Alex's dorm without too much wandering. On the first occasion, over two months ago, I was en route to college, full of optimism about a fresh start on a fresh coast. I had a girlfriend, and I was on my way to study something I actually thought I might be good at.

Look at me now—disillusioned, single, flunking out. And the vending machine business has intruded into my life more than it ever did in all the years I lived at home.

"Vince! What are you doing here?"

The air in the room smells like stale pizza sealed in an ancient tomb. Alex himself is rumpled, harassed, and pathetically happy to see me. I look beyond him and understand why.

On a lacerated vinyl chair that's bleeding fluff lounges a young man built like a bull moose. His months of inactivity as Alex's houseguest have softened his boxer's physique and added a paunch, which bulges out between his tattered T-shirt and gym shorts. No wonder Alex is so intimidated by this guy. He reminds me of so many of the people on the fringes of my father's business. Bland and placid on the surface—like nitro, nothing but a glass of water until you shake it up—then, capable of sudden explosive violence.

And sure enough, he's picking his teeth with a wicked-looking switchblade.

It's to him I address my greeting. "Hi, Tooth-pick."

He jumps, interposing the knife uncomfortably between himself and me. "I think you're mixing me up with somebody else. Name's Frankie Toronto, pal."

I'm amazed that I'm not more scared right now. Maybe I'm getting used to dealing with these wiseguys. Maybe last night's shootout toughened me up. Or maybe I just know that I've got the ulti-mate weapon printed on my birth certificate.

"I'm Vince Luca," I tell him. "You've probably heard of my father."

He nods silently, his face the color of putty.

Alex is getting nervous. "Vince, what are you doing? Frankie, don't hurt him. He doesn't know what he's saying."

"He's not Frankie," I announce firmly. "His name is Toothpick Anderson, and he used to be the driver for a union boss in L.A.—till he helped some people kidnap the guy. He isn't the houseguest from hell, Alex. He's on the lam here! No one would ever have found him if he didn't pick his teeth."

Toothpick waves the knife. "What do you want? I've already blown the money they paid me."

"I'm doing you a favor," I tell him. "Your old

boss got rescued last night, and a lot of people are looking for you. My dad, for one. This might be a good time to leave the country."

He nods fervently, even appreciatively, but then hesitates. "Why do you care if I get away?"

"I don't want a gunfight in my friend's dorm room. And I also don't want him to end up an accidental witness to—something. You disappearing is the best for everybody."

He pulls a duffel bag out from under the bed and begins stuffing his ratty possessions inside. "It's about time I got out of this sewer anyway."

"It wasn't a sewer till you got here," snaps Alex, gaining in courage now that Toothpick seems to be leaving. He supervises the packing, snatching back any items that belong to him.

The Man Who Wouldn't Leave looks a little contrite. "Nothing personal, kid. You were just at the wrong place at the wrong time. I couldn't lam with Frankie on account of him and Tommy Luca being tight. So when you left that message on his answering machine about being in town, I figured you'd never know I wasn't him."

"It was starting to dawn on me," Alex says sulkily. "A TV-addicted hermit isn't exactly the personality type to be a talent scout for chorus girls."

He laughs. "I just made that up to get into your room. Frankie's not a booking agent, genius; he's a forger! He's wanted in seventeen states for check fraud."

Ka-chunk! That's my sluggish brain shifting gears.

Check fraud. A coincidence? I don't think so.

In an instant, I understand how Tommy got the signatures on the checks that emptied the foreign students' bank accounts.

Frankie the forger.

It doesn't take much detective work. I phone Frankie's number. Tommy answers.

I'm so mad I hang up on him. But Toothpick gives me the address in return for a ride to the bus station. So I'm there, and Frankie lets me in.

"Hey, Vince. It's an honor to meet you. Tommy's in the shower."

"Good." I go to the kitchen sink and turn the cold water on full-blast. Then I flush the toilet in the half bath.

There's a howl of pain from upstairs, and my brother comes roaring down, wrapped in a towel. "Jeez, Frankie, you scalded my—" He catches sight of me. "Oh, hey, Vince. When did you get into town?"

I'm too furious to do anything but yell. "You stole their *grant money*? A bunch of foreign students who are living on instant noodles and Kool-Aid, and giving blood for the free cookies? You bastard! You parasite! You tapeworm!"

Tommy looks wounded. "You've got it all wrong."

"I saw their bank statements! I saw the canceled checks—forged by *him*!" I glare at Frankie.

"This is obviously a family dispute," our host says mildly. "I'm going to take a dip in the pool." He makes himself scarce.

"Did you ever think of Zora?" I round on my brother again. "She was in love with you! But you don't care about that. You've got to have a heart to feel emotion. How about Scooby? He's going to get deported because of you! But, hey, no big whoop. Tommy Luca got *his* share—and everybody else's, too!"

He's getting annoyed. "All right, Vince. That's enough. You know what I do."

"No, I don't!" I rage. "Because you told me you were going straight!"

"I said I was *thinking* about it," he replies. "I thought about it. I decided to do this instead."

"Those kids worshipped you! You were their hero! You've got to give them their money back."

"Hey!" He bristles. "I *earned* that money."

"You mean you stole it!"

"I found an angle," he insists. "That's my job. If I worked at A&P, I'd be bagging groceries. I work for Dad, and there are no do-overs. We don't give refunds. Money is for spending, and for betting, and for kicking upstairs to the bosses, and for putting out on the street to make more money. Period."

And then I have one of my brainstorms—an odd term, since they've obviously got nothing to do with brains. On pure impulse I say, "I'll play you for it."

"Play what?" he snorts. "Candy Land?"

I stick out my jaw. "Blackjack."

He snorts. "You've got nothing to put up."

"My car."

"We're talking fifty large, not fifty cents."

I swallow hard. "Next year's tuition, and the first semester the year after that."

"You're on!"

Shuffling takes half an hour. No trust. All that time, I'm thinking, What am I, crazy? I can just see myself explaining to Anthony Luca that I'm dropping out of school, but he still has to pay eighteen months of tuition to Tommy. That'll go over well. Dad's the one who taught Tommy everything he knows about hanging on to money.

One thing is clear. This is totally for real. In the underworld, a gambling debt is something you honor before you feed your children. If I lose this, I'm on the hook for it. I might owe it to Tommy, or to my father because he paid for me, but I *will* owe it. I'll be the first nonstudent ever to start his adult life struggling under a student loan.

Every molecule of logic screams for me to get out of there before I ruin my life. But my sense of what's fair, and right, and decent keeps my butt in the chair. If it wasn't for me, those foreign students would never have heard the name Tommy Luca. I have to get them their money back.

My high-minded morality has an unlikely ally: pure Luca cussedness. Or, as they call it in the vending machine business, balls. Mine are the size of football helmets right now.

It goes badly from the outset. Tommy pulls two face cards and stands on twenty. I draw a nine and a seven.

"Tough break, Vince," he beams, indicating he doesn't think it's tough at all.

As I stare at the back of the next card in the pile—the one I have to take—the utter mystery that is Mr. Lai's Probability class comes into perfect focus in my mind. There are forty-eight cards left in this deck. Four of them are fives. I have a one-in-twelve chance of drawing one of them. Not great odds, but somehow just understanding it all makes the game seem friendlier, like it's on my side.

"Tell you what," Tommy offers magnanimously. "I'll cut your tab in half if you call it quits right now."

I conjure up my best Luca Stare, and I can tell he sees Dad looking at him out of my eyes. I flip over the next card.

The five of hearts.

To his credit, my brother never even complains. To give away $54,618 is a crime against humanity. To lose it in a card game is all part of The Life.

CHAPTER TWENTY-ONE

On November 1, Representative William Sutter of the thirty-sixth district of California surrenders himself to the authorities. He's charged with union tampering and conspiracy to commit kidnapping.

It's a huge story, carried live on every TV station in town. My dad predicted the whole thing as we said good-bye in front of Shibley Textiles that awful night: "You'll see, Vince. He'll waltz into the police station with no handcuffs, in a suit that costs more than the national debt. If it was one of us, they'd send the SWAT team."

He's right. Felon or not, Trey's dad looks like a million bucks on MSNBC.

Trey is riveted to the screen as he stands at the ironing board, spray-starching his shirt to wear with the Hugo Boss for his father's arraignment. The congressman's dream team of lawyers wants the family on hand to create a wholesome all-American image at the hearing.

"And you're okay with that?" I ask tentatively. Playing congressman's son for the TV cameras is Trey's worst nightmare.

He stares at me. "What are you, crazy? I'll do whatever it takes to prove my dad's innocent!"

I keep my mouth shut. There's plenty of time for him to learn his father is a criminal. Take it from someone who got that education at a very tender age. Trey probably knows it already.

"The cops in this town are totally out of control," Trey goes on. "They can't keep murderers off the street, so they have to make a circus arrest. My dad devoted his life to this lousy burg!"

I guess the city isn't working for Congressman Sutter anymore.

I know that sounds callous, but let's face it: The guy is guilty as sin. If it wasn't for the Lucas, Ellis Rank probably would have ended up dead. Besides, William Sutter isn't exactly facing the gas chamber.

Dad again: "With his squeaky-clean reputation and those Gucci lawyers, he'll get two years less a day at Club Med, and be out in half that. Then what? Community service? He'll paint the orphanage for a few months. He might even get elected again. People are idiots."

Court TV should hire Anthony Luca as an analyst. He certainly has a unique perspective.

"What do you think?" Trey holds the shirt up critically. "Gotta look perfect. When I tell the judge what a great father William Sutter is, he has to believe me."

"Then you might want to cut out the shoplifting," I suggest. "Judges aren't too high on that. Especially when it comes to classic cars."

He's offended by this reference to his old hobby. "Like I'd risk my dad's future for some tin-plated crapmobile!" All at once, the iron hits the floor, and Trey is gawking at the screen. "Vince! It's *him*!"

"The iron!" I have to rush over and rescue it from a cloud of steam. "Watch it! That thing could burn through to Perry's room!"

"It's *him*," he repeats. "The old geezer who's dating Willow! He's on TV!"

"Where?" And when I follow his pointing finger to the middle-aged man in the crowd around Congressman Sutter at central booking, my shock is far greater than Trey's.

I recognize this guy. No, that's not strong

enough. I *know* him. I've had dinner at his table.

It's Agent Bite-Me.

"Trey!" I blurt in my astonishment. "That's Kendra's father!"

"Kendra's father is dating Willow?"

"Kendra's father is FBI!" I explain breathlessly. "He's the agent who's after my dad. Don't you get it? If Willow was meeting an FBI agent behind a Dumpster, she's working for the feds too—posing undercover as a student!"

He's confused. "Why would the FBI put a mole inside a college?"

"To get to the son of a congressman they suspect of union tampering. Willow practically threw herself at you, remember? Then, when she found out who *I* was, she realized that my dad's an even bigger fish. So who does she talk to? The agent in charge of the Luca case. And pretty soon, she's coming on to me."

It's pretty slick, actually. Entrapping a guy with a beautiful girl is standard procedure in the underworld. But I never thought my own government would stoop to it. It says something about Agent Bite-Me—if you live long enough, you become what you despise most. Or maybe it just shows that he's learned more from all those wiretaps than what Mom was cooking for dinner.

"We got *used* by a hot FBI agent!" Trey marvels. "How cool is that?"

Cool for him. This episode cost me my girlfriend. I'll bet Kendra's dear old dad was only too happy to show her those beach pictures. Breaking the two of us up was always a higher priority for the guy than shutting down Anthony Luca.

However, stewing on that subject, or any other, is something I just don't have time for. Once again, I'm behind the eight ball in TV production class. My next video is due in three days, and I haven't even given a thought to the topic. I don't blame myself—I've been pretty busy. But I've used up all my brownie points with Mr. Baumgartner. In the time it's taken me to arrive at progress point zero, everybody else in class has completed two full projects, and P-Rick has written, shot, and edited an entire musical comedy that's more than an hour long.

Then, a ray of hope. It comes as I'm giving the foreign students their grant money back, counting out wads of cash from a paper grocery sack. Scooby is so grateful that he can now pay his tuition and stay in the country that he presents me with a gift: two hours of videotape. It starts when I almost ran him over on Lincoln Boulevard, and ends on Trey's suicide run with the VW bus.

"I can't accept this," I tell him. "It's your work, not mine."

"Oh, no," he insists. "I see none of this, I shoot nothing if you do not take me. I am the cameraman only. You are the director."

It's true. In film and TV, the body behind the camera is only a tool. The writer, actors, crew— same thing. The ultimate author of a piece is always the director.

So now I've got a mission. I have to take two hours of raw footage into the editing room and tell a story with it.

What I see on that small screen astounds me. Normally, Scooby's endless documentary is worse than boring. But the stuff in the warehouse is pure gold. There are so many things I didn't notice when it was happening in real life. Like the look on my father's face when he realizes that I'm there, standing in what will soon be the line of fire. Or the shootout itself. I remember it as the OK Corral, but there were exactly four shots fired. Four too many, yes. But only four.

Most surprising of all, when I start to cut my project together, I realize that I'm actually enjoying this, and maybe even showing kind of a knack for it.

In TV production class, we draw straws for

screening order, and I get the spot nobody wants, right after P-Rick. But *Burnt Offering* turns out to be kind of a flop—not funny enough to be a comedy, but too intentionally dumb to work as a biblical epic. And the music is no better than mediocre.

Of course, I'm glued to the screen, clinging to Kendra like a shipwrecked sailor to a piece of flotsam. This will probably be the last chance I ever get to watch her perform. Somehow, I transfer all my bittersweet emotions and regrets to the video. I'm almost as surprised as P-Rick himself that nobody else liked it.

Then it's time for *The Warehouse*. After an hour of biblical farce shot in cloudless daylight, the images seem stark and high contrast. The editing is rapid-fire, giving the piece a pounding, relentless pace.

It gets rapt attention from the class, followed by a standing ovation. Even P-Rick is on his feet. Mr. Baumgartner is so moved that he hugs me.

"I'm speechless!" he declares, and then goes on to blab about my video for twenty minutes. "There's a galvanizing realism to the action. The tough guy who jumps on you is a little disappointing. He's a bit of a caricature. But I loved the chaotic camera movement during the shootout sequence. And that scene with the Volkswagen bus—how did you manage it? It really looks like the entire front end was smashed in. Congratulations!"

"Thank you," I say faintly. I wonder how Anthony Luca would feel if I told him that he's not a believable Mob boss.

"We're going to keep working on this, Vince," the teacher vows. "A few more hours in the editing room, and I'll be proud to enter *The Warehouse* in the student video competition at the Sundance Film Festival."

Okay, I know. I'm getting complimented for all the wrong reasons. But right now it just feels good to not suck at something.

Things are looking up on other fronts as well. Even in Probability class, my designated clunker, I ace the latest test.

"It's a remarkable transformation," Mr. Lai praises me. "That's the alchemy of education. Who knows what makes a concept mysteriously click in a student's mind?"

I don't say it out loud, but I know exactly when I began to understand probability. Las Vegas, Nevada, in Frankie the forger's kitchen, when the money suddenly became real.

* * *

There's a spring in my step on the way home. It's seventy-two degrees, the morning haze has burned off, and at that moment, Santa Monica seems like a pretty good place to be. California—so this is what all the fuss is about.

INT. MAYER HALL—THE LOBBY—DAY

STUDENTS are everywhere in the crowded atrium, standing in groups, and draped over couches and chairs. . . .

TRACKING SHOT—VINCE'S P.O.V.

The camera pans from FACE to FACE before settling on . . .

KENDRA, in the back by the mailboxes.

VINCE tucks his book bag in the crook of his arm and barrels across the lobby, knocking down anyone who gets in his way. He scoops up KENDRA in a soulful embrace.

The STUDENTS cheer.

ROLL CREDITS on HAPPY ENDING.

Okay, it doesn't happen that way. But she's

there. Not to see P-Rick. Not to rehearse. That's over now. HAPPY ENDING may be premature, but her presence has ONE MORE CHANCE written all over it.

"She was an agent, Kendra," I say. "And your dad could probably tell you that she specializes in guys like me."

She nods. "I know."

I'm surprised. "How?"

"I never would have figured it out," she concedes. "I was so mad, I never wanted to see you again. It was Richard who set me straight. He said, how could a twenty-one-year-old goddess like Willow fall for a guy like Vince?"

I'm offended. "Oh, right. And I'm sure P-Rick has a line-up of Victoria's Secret models clamoring for a piece of his flabby butt."

"Are you kidding?" she asks. "Have you seen his girlfriend?"

"I've never found those blow-up dolls to look very realistic."

"Don't be mean. He has her picture in his wallet. She's gorgeous!"

Okay, so P-Rick knows how to use PhotoShop Deluxe to insert Reese Witherspoon into his prom snapshot. Big deal. Alex thought of that two years ago. "Well, anyway, I'm glad you listened to him,"

I say aloud. "Because, in this case, he happens to be right."

"I didn't take his word for it," she admits. "I squeezed the truth out of my father. He still loves me more than he hates you."

I avoid her eyes. "I never should have let things go so far with Willow. I'm not perfect."

"Me neither," she says fervently. "I was nuts to think I could keep up with school, have a relationship, and still be in *Burnt Offering*. Richard's brilliant, but he's a slave driver."

"The reviews have been kind of mixed so far. Not for you," I add quickly. "You stole the show. The desert suits you. Beige is your color."

She makes a face. "Snakes all over the place. You can never get the dust out of your hair. And the people! We were out by Riverside filming the sacrifice, and some lady called the cops on us. She thought we were a satanic cult."

I nod sympathetically. "Showbiz." I'm not sure exactly when it happens, but her arms are around my neck, and mine are around her waist. Imperfect we may be, but we're perfect together.

God, I'm easy.

We get snickered at in the elevator, and Kendra goes all shy on me. Call me crazy, but I kind of like it. I think of Willow, so self-assured, aggressive, and competent. There's no denying her skill; every move smooth, every touch just so. But what Kendra and I have is better. It seems somehow right that we bumble through this like the amateurs we are, making it up as we go along.

Finally, the fourth floor. She pushes me into the bell-tower stairwell. "We've got some catching up to do."

"You picked a good time," I inform her. "I happen to be the toast of campus these days. A week ago, I was toe jam; now I've got a video that's going to be entered at Sundance."

She's excited. "That should have been the first thing you said to me! That's awesome! Can I see it?"

"Actually, you can't," I reply. "And I can't explain why, either." I regard her nervously. This is usually when the trouble starts.

She kisses me so suddenly that I keel over backward on the steps. She falls on top of me, and I lock my arms around her. This is a moment that has been building between us for two solid months. I've anticipated it, dreamed about it, suffered for it, and grieved that it would never come. I'm not letting go.

If you think the bell-tower stairs are steep and claustrophobic, you should try to navigate them backward while joined at the lips. At the fifth floor we almost kill ourselves over Calvin's telescope. Even then, we only interrupt our make-out session long enough for Kendra to right the instrument on its stool, and point the lens at the correct window.

I'm already reaching for her when she frowns into the eyepiece. "That guy up there—he looks kind of familiar. Isn't he someone famous?"

A second later I'm peering through the glass at the condo across the way—and the unmistakable features of former Beatles' drummer Ringo Starr.

I thought no power in this world could detour me from my goal of getting Kendra behind the locked door of room 601. I was wrong.

"Calvin! Perry! Get out here! *Now!*"

The celebration is like Mardi Gras—Calvin, his face pink, punching at the air, bellowing, *"Rock and roll!"*; Mitch slapping high fives; the stunned Anorexia, repeating, "I didn't believe you guys," over and over; her sister and Perry, their feud temporarily suspended, hugging each other a little too tightly to be explained by this blessed event. Even P-Rick comes down to check it out. It's almost as if the guy has a clue. I guess I'll have to get used to the idea of not hating him. He's an idiot, but he did save my relationship with Kendra.

Only Trey is absent. He's been spending all his time attending legal strategy sessions with his father and the dream team. They're at a marathon brainstorming today. I tip an imaginary Bad Shark hat to him. Sorry you missed it, *hombre*.

Some kids from the fourth floor straggle up the steps to investigate the source of the noise. By this time, we're belting out a chorus of "Octopus's Garden." They look at us like we're nuts. Maybe Perry's right—there's something about life in the bell tower that the trogs will never understand.

Across the street, Ringo himself gives a perfunctory wave and turns his back on us. He's lived through Beatlemania. Our disturbance is nothing special. Following his lead, I grab Kendra's hand, and we discreetly exit the party and sneak upstairs.

I'm surprised to find the door to 601 unlocked and slightly ajar.

I frown. "Trey?"

No answer.

Oh, please don't let it be Uncle Uncle stopping by to make another statement! I peer into the bathroom. Empty.

And then my eyes travel to where I know they should, and see something I knew they would.

The videotape of *The Warehouse* is gone from my desk. In its place sits a Tupperware container.

I crack the lid and take a whiff. Pesto ravioli—Mom's special recipe.

And the amazing part? I'm not even that upset. The minute I watched that footage, I realized Anthony Luca was never going to let it live. Hey, this is a guy who wouldn't even allow a top captain's wife to film a pool party. In the heat of the moment, with bullets flying and his son in harm's way, he may not have noticed Scooby's tiny Palmcorder. But the minute he found out that that cassette existed, it was gone. To Dad, videotape will always be evidence, and evidence will always be something you get rid of—even when it shows you being the good guys.

That's why I never allowed myself to get too excited about Sundance. I don't count my chickens when I know they're never going to be hatched.

Poor Mr. Baumgartner. This is probably going to kill him.

Kendra sees me with the Tupperware. "Smells great. What is it?"

I shrug. "My video project."

When I explain it to her, she's appalled. "Vince, this is crazy! How can you let your father destroy what might turn out to be your first big break?"

I'm tempted to point out that her own father has spent the better part of a decade trying to thwart Anthony Luca, without much success. What makes her think I would fare any better?

But I don't say anything. Trey is away, the room is ours, and Kendra and I are back together again. This city has finally started working for me.

Dad has a slightly different perspective on the videotape issue.

"*The Godfather*, *Goodfellas*, *The Sopranos*—" he tells me the next time I phone home. "A million books and movies, and still nobody understands what it's really about. And I'm sure as hell not going to put it right up there on the screen at some film festival."

"I never even watched the final cut all the way through," I complain.

I can almost hear the grin. "Tell you what, Steven Spielberg. When you come home for Thanksgiving, we'll have our own film festival."

"You kept it?" I ask in amazement. This is *videotape*. And it shows not only his people but himself in action.

"Of course!" he exclaims. "Brilliant new director. Kid named Luca."